# THE SNUGGLY
# SIRENICON

Brian Stableford's scholarly work includes *New Atlantis: A Narrative History of Scientific Romance* (Wildside Press, 2016), T*he Plurality of Imaginary Worlds: The Evolution of French roman scientifique* (Black Coat Press, 2017) and *Tales of Enchantment and Disenchantment: A History of Faerie* (Black Coat Press, 2019). In support of the latter projects he has translated more than a hundred volumes of roman scientifique and more than twenty volumes of contes de fées into English. He has edited *Decadence and Symbolism: A Showcase Anthology* (Snuggly Books, 2018), and is busy translating more Symbolist and Decadent fiction.

His recent fiction, in the genre of metaphysical fantasy, includes a trilogy of novels set in West Wales, consisting of *Spirits of the Vasty Deep* (2018), *The Insubstantial Pageant* (2018) and *The Truths of Darkness* (2019), published by Snuggly Books, and a trilogy set in Paris and the south of France, consisting of *The Painter of Spirits*, *The Quiet Dead* and *Living with the Dead*, all published by Black Coat Press in 2019.

I0591621

# THE SNUGGLY
# SIRENICON

EDITED, INTRODUCED AND TRANSLATED BY

BRIAN STABLEFORD

THIS IS A SNUGGLY BOOK

Translations and Introduction
Copyright © 2021 by Brian Stableford.
All rights reserved.

ISBN: 978-1-64525-078-4

# CONTENTS

# INTRODUCTION

THIS volume is a sequel of sorts to *The Snuggly Satyricon*, which was a book of satyrs. The present volume is a book of sirens—or, more pedantically, *sirènes*—as that word was understood in a particular phase of French literary history. Like the notion of the satyr, the notion of sirens was taken up with particular relish by writers who described themselves as Symbolists, having picked up the torch of French Romanticism in order to carry forward its quest to defend fertile, inventive and richly meaningful imagination against the corrosions of positivistic thought.

By the time the litterateurs featured in this Sirenicon took up the notion of the mythological siren, the meaning of the word had already been hijacked. Originally, sirens were chimerical compounds of humans and birds, with feathers, wings and avian feet. Not necessarily female to begin with, the notion soon developed that they were all female and probably not very numerous, three being the quantity most often cited; their invariable key feature was, however, that they had beautiful, seductive and treacherous voices, which lured men to their doom. They were routinely alleged to live on islands and to direct their treachery against seamen, which doubtless aided in their eventual metamorphosis into chimerical compounds of human and fish, most frequently into the stereotyped "mermaid" in which the upper body of a beautiful woman is fused with the hindquarters and tail of a fish.

By the time the stories in the present Sirenicon were written, the mermaid had become the archetypal image of a siren in French literature, although, like any imaginary species, it was subject to variation at whim. Its usurpation of the older image was undoubtedly helped by the fact that in the most famous encounters with the sirens described in Classical literature, in the *Odyssey* and the *Argonautica*, the sirens are only heard and not seen, their form remaining unspecified. Sirens of that sort were not unrivaled in French fiction of the late nineteenth century; naiads and undines still retained a certain venerability from the days when they featured routinely on the margins of *contes de fées*, and Germanic Rhine-Maidens—along with their clones, nixies and lorelei—had received a significant boost from Wagnermania, but in the main, mermaiden sirens occupied the center.

The stories in the present collection were written at a time when the idea that sirens of the semipiscine variety might really exist was not quite extinct. Nineteenth-century newspapers still featured occasional articles about "real" (i.e., imaginary) mermaid sightings, and sometimes offered elaborate accounts of the history of such sightings culled from earlier reports, the accumulation of which seemed to lend them a gloss of plausibility. Fake mermaids were so commonplace in eighteenth- and nineteenth-century cabinets of curiosities that their manufacture became a significant cottage industry in the Low Countries, accommodated to the more general category of strategically modified marine animals known as "Jenny Hanivers."

The most elaborate French literary account of a strangely seductive siren, *Les Mariages du père Olifus* (1849; tr. as *The Man who Married a Mermaid*), originally credited to Alexandre Dumas but mostly written by Pierre Lacroix, alias "P. L. Jacob the Bibliophile," contains a prefatory chapter offering a long list alleged sightings of mermaids and a trip to see a supposed museum specimen. Censors of the imagination, always eager to misconstrue invention as stupidity, often credited such eye-witness accounts to the mistaken perception of animals such as seals and sea-cows, and biological taxonomists, always great punsters, created an order of Sirenia to contain dugongs and manatees, as well as dubbing a family of aquatic salamanders Sirenidae.

Within the tradition of French philosophical thought, reported sightings of "aquatic humans" also played a significant role in the work of the first great evolutionist, Benoît de Maillet, who proposed in the early eighteenth century, on the basis of geological evidence, that all life had begun in the sea and must have evolved gradually to live on land as previously-submerged continents emerged therefrom. Required by that thesis to imagine a process of gradual metamorphosis by which marine creatures such as fish had eventually produced humankind, he used reportage of ambiguous creatures, including mermaids, to support his thesis. Hardly anyone took him seriously—mostly for reasons of religious bigotry, the devout being horrified by his heresy—but his notion was taken up and extensively developed by the radical philosopher and prolific writer of fiction Nicolas Edmé Restif de la Bretonne, most extravagantly in *La Découverte australe par un homme-volant, ou Le Dédale française* (1781; tr. as *The Discovery of the Austral Continent by a Flying Man; or, The French Dedalus*) and *La Philosophie de Monsieur Nicolas* (1796). Although largely forgotten by the time the stories in the present collection were written, those evolutionist ideas were not devoid of an imaginative legacy, and the thinking behind them is echoed in several of the stories, sometimes in a curious amalgam that the fuses the nostalgia of extinct myths with the nostalgia of extinct species.

In her essence, the siren is an archetype of the *femme fatale*: the seductive female who lures men irresistibly to destruction. In that, she is a counterpart of sorts to the satyr, the personification of male carnal lust. Whereas the nymphs typically pursued by satyrs and fauns are usually construed as helpless potential victims, whose only possible escape from violation is magical metamorphosis, sirens are merciless exploiters of male lust, nymphomorphic decoys who employ their inherent attractiveness to trap luckless victims of their hormones, like the praying mantis of modern biological legend who beheads and eats the male of her species while sexual intercourse leaves him defenseless and enraptured. Typical of writers working in the Romantic tradition, however, the litterateurs in the present collection often reconfigure the siren sympathetically, pleading her innocence—because she is, after all, unable to help the effect she has on men—and representing her as repenting of, or at least regretting, its lethality.

That kind of sympathy is mostly an aspect of male wishful thinking rather than feminist suspicion, and one of the two female writers represented in the present collection, Renée Vivien, who often employed her work to celebrate Sapphic lust, elects to use a narrative voice that identifies with entranced hearers of the siren song rather than with its singers. The other, Lucie Delarue-Mardrus, who was, like Renée Vivien, a member of Natalie Barney's coterie, adopts the hypothetical viewpoint of the siren for an exercise in misandry more flamboyantly pointed than the misanthropism exhibited in some of the other narratives.

With regard to sentimental sympathy for the siren, the French writers included here had a far more influential model than the domestically-produced novella by Dumas and Lacroix, in the story that has become one of the great archetypes of modern literary mythology, Hans Christian Andersen's "Den lille Havfrue" (1837; tr. into English as "The Little Mermaid" and into French as "La Petite sirène"). The idea of a siren who is bewitched by human male beauty, sacrifices her immortality in order to follow its lure, and obtains legs at the cost of always feeling that she is walking upon sharp knives, offers a flamboyant exercise in hypothetical role-reversal, inevitably tempting to the male ego, which is typically vicious and cruel although generally clad in a fur-coated armor of hypocrisy. It is echoed in more than one of the stories herein—Maurice Magre's "The Flower of Youth" is clearly partially inspired by it—but its example is perhaps even more important as a provocation of perverse dissent than as an inspiration to imitation. Given the period in which they were written, it is not surprising that the stores feature at least as many cynical *hommes fatales* as treacherous *femmes fatales*.

Even more so than the notion of the satyr, the notion of the siren separates the depiction of carnal pursuit from that of consummation. If satyrs actually catch the nymphs they pursue, the outcome is usually a tragic violation. On the other hand, even if an enticed male is fortunate enough to find a sympathetic and kindly siren, it is profoundly unclear what they are actually going to do together, the piscine lower abdomen presumably lacking the hospitable sexual equipment necessary for comfortable intercourse. Fortunately—or not—decency forbids that difficulty actually to be spelled out, even in the minority of stories where a solution seems to be found to it. There is not a single story here that makes the explicit suggestion, perhaps obvious to the twenty-first century eye, that mermaids are at least capable of oral intercourse (although whether their partners can return the compliment remains an intriguing moot point). Romantically inclined stories settle instead for the rather unconvincing argument that if underwater intercourse with a siren is bound to be fatal, then it must surely be the best death available to a sensitive young man who finds life on land too arid.

"The Little Mermaid" was not the only story of foreign origin to make a considerable impact on the French literary imagination, but the other, H. G. Wells's *The Sea Lady* (1902; tr. into French as *Miss Waters*, 1906) did not arrive soon enough to influence most of the authors featured in the present collection. André Lichtenberger's parody of Wells, however, "Mr. Cuffycoat's Adventure," is an interesting synthesis of French and English attitudes, which adds a useful note to the chorus of voices, even though it has to be reckoned something of an afterthought. In that, it is not out of line with the earlier stories, all of which tend to see their own representations of sirens as afterthoughts, dealing with an image already certified as obsolete. The collection contains four stories entitled "The Last Siren" and several more dealing with alleged relics of a species already extinct; the few stories that allege that sirens might still exist and might continue to do so make their argument defensively, and not merely as a reaction to the dominance of popular cynicism regarding newspaper reportage of "actual" sightings. There is a sense in which siren stories of the late nineteenth and early twentieth centuries are haunted by the idea that they are trafficking with a myth further past its sell-by date than many other hypothetical creatures, some of which had yet to reach their peak of literary fashionability—vampires and werewolves are obvious examples.

That notion of obsolescence is assisted by the dramatic implausibility of the image, far more radical than the combination of human and goat making up a satyr, or even the combination of human and horse making up a centaur. In spite of Benoît de Maillet's propagandizing of a biological kinship, the two halves of a mermaid are clearly much more distantly related than purely mammalian mosaics. And yet, the image does have a certain innate fascination that is difficult of explanation, which extends to such kindred figures as the legendary "fay" Melusine whose lower half was required to turn into an ophidian or piscine form once a week while she bathed—a figure sufficiently commonplace in literary fantasies almost to qualify as a microsubgenre in her own right. The present collection is, however, more tightly focused, only including stories in which the term *sirène* is actually used.

As with the *Satyricon* that preceded it, the *Sirenicon* obviously takes the risk of monotony, and it is arguable that there is some repetition here, but as with the earlier volume, the consistency of the core image permits the variations to stand out more sharply and to recommend themselves for comparison and contrast. Many of the writers, aware of the fact that they are working within a microsubgenre, actually strive conscientiously to import difference into their stories, feeling more pressure to seek originality than would be required if they were working with a less stereotyped motif. The collection illustrates the remarkable effects that that kind of spur can have, in such highly distinctive and effective stories as Pierre Mille's "The Sirens" and Camille Lemmonier's "The Woman of the Sea," but it also adds an extra quality of sensitivity to the work of staunchly traditional writers like Paul Arène, in his delicate exercises in "fakelore." Like the earlier collection, this is something of an experiment, the success of which might be judged differently by different readers, but the inherent fascination of the motif will hopefully ensure that it is anything but tedious.

—Bran Stableford

14

# THE SNUGGLY
# SIRENICON

# SIRENS' CREEK

## by Paul Arène

IN my walks around the cape, I sometimes slowed my pace at that spot in order to listen to a veritably strange music.

In the periods when the mistral reigns, when the waves roll from the azure, and caper, crazy rather than irritated, under the clear sky in the intoxication and the light of a tempest in bright sunlight, one might have thought that somewhere between the rocks there was the endless lamentation of prisoners or the damned.

At other times, when the sea is appeased in order to cradle more softly and more blue the nest that a bird confides to it, during the long calms that were once called halcyon days, it was with crystal vibrations, caresses and sighs, like a chorus of feminine voices: a delectably sacrilegious evocation, simultaneously pagan and mystical, voluptuous and mortuary, of virgins sobbing over the tomb of Adonis, or canticles heard on holy Thursday behind the curtains of veiled oratories, amid the perfumes of incense and the palpitations of candles.

But whether the wind was blowing or not, sometimes plaintive and sometimes rebellious, the same harmony always rose up distinctly at the same place, without it being possible to confuse it with the other cries and plaints of the sea.

One morning, I wanted to know. So, leaving the stony path that wound through myrtles and dwarf tamarisks along the steep coast, I set forth bravely into the rocks.

By virtue of the dispositions of my soul, that somewhat infantile expedition immediately appeared to me to have something mysterious about it.

The solitude was complete. By my side, there was nothing but my shadow; in the distance, a unique living dot, motionless in the blue of the sky or descending to brush the blue waves with its oblique wing, the seagull with nacreous pinions that Apuleius, instead of the classical doves, gives for a confidant and messenger to the Mediterranean Aphrodite.

And everywhere, in the rocks, white under the sun, under the mirror of the infinite sea, there were dreams and visions; for, as much as the night, the divine light has its phantoms, sphinxes, chimeras or sirens, which the eyes of the Greeks really saw.

A surprise awaited me. Although the route was inconvenient over the sharp crests and trenchant ridges of a marmoreal limestone, so bizarrely corroded by the spray and the sunlight that it was comparable to petrifications of foam, I did not regret my fit of curiosity for long.

The voices persisted, guiding me, increasingly characteristic and sonorous. Now, although the rigid wall of the cliff where the waves break was a few paces further away, by virtue of a strange auditory hallucination, I seemed to hear them beneath my feet.

Suddenly, they burst forth. From the midst of the arid rocks, a light smoke rose up, followed by a jet of foaming water, the splashing pearls of which rebounded as far as me.

Then, looking over a fallen boulder at the place from which that pagan baptism was coming, I perceived, regularly sculpted as if by a chisel, a kind of rectangular well with damp walls covered with shellfish, fucus and floating anemones.

In the depths of the well, a narrower opening allowed a glimpse, down below, of scintillation of deep green water. And I was saying, pursuing my dream: "That's certainly an ideal retreat for marine divinities," when I saw a wave bound through the narrow opening with a louder rumble and fill the well with a white spray, which inundated me for a second time.

Evidently, there was a grotto there, communicating with the sea by invisible vents, in which the water, retained prisoner, rose or descended in accordance with the tide.

And, recalling—why had those details not struck me sooner?—that on old maps the place was named Sirens' Creek or Serene Creek, and that the local fishermen still call the ensemble of rocks that make up the cyclopean rim of the well Altar Rock, I started thinking that on the white promontory that once rose there, with its altar, as in Sorrento, there must have been a temple dedicated to the irresistible and cruel deities by some Tyrian navigator or Greek adventurer—perhaps Ulysses, going astray in those unknown seas. Then, in the depths of the somber sanctuary, as today in the bright sunlight, through the narrow vent, the song of the sirens rose up and the initiates, inclining, came to listen to their oracle.

Later, the altar having disappeared and the temple forgotten, torn away by the assault of the waves, the frail marble columns collapsed, and nothing any longer remains of that past, near the mysterious hole where an echo of fateful voices still resonates, but a name, Altar Rock, which the fishermen repeat without understanding it.

I was wrong to incriminate the fishermen.

The people, infatuated with illusions, never forget the gods they loved, and retain through the centuries an obscurely grateful soul.

This is what an old fisherman told us about Altar Rock no later than the day before yesterday, in a beached boat, while, on plates of cork-oak bark, with large Golfe Juan scallop-shells for spoons, we were swallowing the golden slices of a magisterial bouillabaisse grouped around a gigantic stove, a masterpiece of potters of Vallauris—a volume of more than twenty-five liters!—possessed today by the brave Saint-Aygous, the last survivor and sole heir of six legendary captains.

He told us that once, "in the time of the Consuls," as they say, all of the Antiboise coast from La Salisse to La Garoupe, because of its creeks fringed with a sand that was always warm and its grottoes shaded by the dark foliage of pines, was extraordinarily abundant in sirens. One saw fish-women everywhere playing on the waves or sun-bathing between the rocks, malevolent for poor folk and yet damnably beautiful with their pointed breasts and their hair woven with coral, so long that it hid the silver scales of their tails. Nests of them were found in spring in the hollows where the sea remains, and although people hastened to destroy them, the sirens pullulated regardless.

Only taking pleasure in malice, however, they did not forgive anyone and attracted into frightful shipwrecks miscreants as well as Christians, the tartans of brethren devoted to Saint Peter as well as Barbary feluccas.

The worst thing of all was that, being daughters of the devil, Saint Peter and the other saints could do nothing against them, apparently not knowing the words necessary to exorcize them.

Fortunately, the reign of the fays arrived in the meantime. Two of them arrived in the country, Esterelle and Morgane, both benefactresses, Morgane for the sea and Esterelle for the mountains.

Esterelle and Morgane agreed to deliver the land from the Sirens. One evening, Morgane attracted all of them into one of the marvelous castles that she was able to build with the sea mist; then, Esterelle having changed the mist into rock, it was a sealed grotto in which the Sirens remained imprisoned.

Since then, when the sea rumbles, clinging to the narrow vent through which light reaches them, they make a racket in order to escape; at other times, hoping to bewitch someone as they once did, they sing in a sweet voice, for if someone ever loves them, the grotto will vanish in smoke and the charm will be broken . . .

"Next month," said Guillamon, one of the guests to whom that tale had seemed interesting, "one could, one afternoon of sea-urchin fishing, try to penetrate that grotto by diving."

His friend Roiouffe approved strongly, and we were about to decide on the adventure when Saint-Aygous, whose nasal voice often speaks wisely, proclaimed: "Halt! It's a matter of going to liberate the sirens? Don't be stupid, my lads, and let's leave those young folk tranquil. It seems to me, thank God, that with women we already have a pretty enough plague of that sort on land!"

# THE LAST SIREN

## by Pierre Mille

A S Christmas draws near, little wooden shops spring up everywhere in Paris on the sidewalks of the boulevards. The most beautiful and most expensive are between the Madeleine and the Rue Drouet; but others, more modest and sometimes singular, go down as far as the Bastille and then flow back along the Rue Saint-Antoine and the Rue de Rivoli to join those of the Sebasto. It was there, on a certain day in December last year that, on the door of the humblest of those stalls, close to the railings of the Square Saint-Jacques, I was able to read on a strip of calico: *A Wonder of the World: the Last Siren.*

It only cost four sous to see it, the last siren, in spite of the cost of living! And the stall wasn't even a hut but an enclosure made of four intersecting planks lined with baling cloth and protected above from the rain by four meters of old bitumen-covered cardboard.

I poured my two ten-centime coins into the hand of a dirty Megaera whose breasts were sagging underneath an old smock. That the siren, the wonder of the world, had simply been stuffed and posed on a plinth of black wood, did not cause me to experience any disappointment. What surprised me, on the contrary, in spite of everything, was the strangeness of that dead thing, its human appearance, its appearance, truly, of a woman terminated by a fish's tail, with a fish's fins—or rather those of a sea-lion or a manatee. But it was neither a sea-lion nor a manatee: no animal teats, but two round firm breasts; breasts that were not even tapering like those of young negresses, European breasts that would not have dishonored the statue of a Greek virgin; a face scarcely less oval than the majority of human faces in our race, with a rather long, well-marked, almost straight nose; very long hair, slightly curly, divided by a natural parting in the middle of a slightly sloping forehead, but high enough. The monster's large orbits, which presented a certain poignant, disquieting beauty, looked straight ahead; they did not diverge like those of animals; excessively brown eyes had been embedded in them on the cheap: vulgar globes of glass.

The people around me were unimpressed, but slightly shaken nevertheless by the strangeness and unexpectedness of that vision; then they joked, by reaction; nothing is more natural. They sought to explain it; no one nowadays wants to believe any longer in miracles. They said to the exhibitor of the "curiosity," a thin, ageing man with the face of an alcoholic mariner: "You've stuffed a negress whom you've cut in half at the waist and then you've adapted another skin to it, the skin of a large fish, perhaps a seal, in order to make the tail. It's not bad!"

The man said nothing. He seemed brutalized, or incredibly sad—one never can tell . . .

I went out, incredulous but nevertheless preoccupied. All evening, the memory of that absurd, implausible being, haunted me. Involuntarily, I went back the following morning to wander around the Square Saint-Jacques. The man was sweeping in front of his cabin; he had no clients at that hour. I went in again. Inside, the fat woman who had been collecting the money the day before was shelling haricot beans in front of the siren. She seemed to me to be even uglier and dirtier than the day before.

The man joined me. He grunted, in an almost inarticulate voice: "You interested . . . ?"

"Let's go have a drink," I said, adeptly.

He shrugged his shoulders and followed me to a bar. He drank several glasses one after another. His eyes became less dull. He repeated several times "You interested . . . ? You interested . . . ?" and then began to talk in little short sentences, mingled with long silences.

"It's true, it's true, the siren! It isn't a fake. It's true! This is how it happened.

"I was fishing with a net with a mate on the Somali coast in the Red Sea, on account of the governor of Djibouti. Monsieur Bonhour, his name was. He was doing research in natural history, that governor. He was studying with a microscope a sort of jelly that was sometimes brought up from the bottom."

"Plankton?" I asked.

"Perhaps . . . don't know. And one night, the net became heavy, very heavy . . . which nearly capsized the boat, or rather the two pirogues, for there were two

25

pirogues, connected by a pole, in the fashion of the country. I thought it was a bonita or a dolphin—there are heaps of them in the Red Sea—that had been caught. We pulled and pulled with the strength of four arms, and we brought it up, the siren! She was weeping like a woman, a real woman; she was afraid! The siren, I tell you, such as she is in my stall, but much more beautiful! If you'd seen her eyes and the beautiful quivering of her breasts! My mate, who was called . . . no, I won't tell you his name, I have my reasons . . . half-stunned her with a blow of the oar on the head.

"I said to him: 'You've hurt her!'

"She had uttered a loud scream and was no longer moving. The mate said: 'It's in order to have her! She was about to get away!'

"We hauled her into the boat, and after a little while she came round. She didn't say anything—nothing we could understand—only rather soft moans. It's a lie, it appears, that they sing, these fish-women. In any case, she never sang in front of me. But it really was a fish-woman, and stark naked, naturally. We looked at one another. The first idea that came to us was 'Half each'. Later, we only wanted half each!

"The mate said: 'Not necessary to take her to the governor in Djibouti; he'd keep her! Necessary to go to the other coast, we'll run aground on the sand. Then we'll take her to Aden in a vat; she needs water to live, I think. From there to Europe, where we'll sell her to scientists. It's rare, that, it's dear.'

"I was agreeable. And while waiting to sell her . . . I thought! They're animals, these sirens, in spite of looking like women. They don't have motives for refusing . . ."

26

"No, no, she didn't have motives for refusing! But when I arrived in Aden with her, it was only with her skin. She was dead, you understand, dead! She hadn't been able to live outside the sea. And I took her skin off. Oh, not to make money, at first, but as one conserves the skin of an animal one has loved, a good dog. She was no longer frightened at all, in the last days. A tender good dog, who might have been a woman."

"But what about the other, your mate?" I asked.

"That's not your business," he said, looking away. "That doesn't concern you, see! He stayed out there, on the sand . . . he . . . didn't come back . . ."

My eyes lowered toward his enormous, hairy, clenched hands. I understood.

"In sum," I concluded, "he's dead, like the siren."

"It's not him that I regret, good God! But when I introduced her to the scientists, in France, the siren, they laughed. They made fun of me. They said: 'Oh, that trick's already been tried on us. It's like rats with trunks and sea-serpents, fabricated with several skins stuck together. They don't exist, sirens, my good man."

"That was it. Then I showed her in a booth; it was two sous before the war, four sous now . . .'

The filthy fat woman who lived with him went past on the sidewalk, a string bag full of leeks in her hand. The man shook his fist.

"And to think that it's not her who's dead! When one thinks! When one thinks!"

And I realized that he would never console himself for having possessed the impossible, for having committed murder for the impossible, and for having lost it.

# THE CANTATRICE

## *by Maurice Renard*

OLD HAUVAL—who is still the director of the Opéra-Dramatique—smoothed his flowing beard with a gnarled hand and said: "This is what happened!"

In 189*, in the month of March, there was a performance of *Siegfried* at Monte Carlo. An extraordinary interpretation made that revival the great lyrical event of the season. I had decided to see it, and I left Paris with a group of artistes, critics and dilettantes who were racing, without knowing it, to the most troubling auditory experience that living men might undergo. I shall spare you the vicissitudes of the journey, for our journey was nothing but vicissitudes: pauses, delays, and a forced two-hour halt in Marseilles caused by a railway accident, which I employed as best I could in visiting the city. Suffice it to say that I went, reached Monaco, and arrived at the performance.

It commenced in splendor and continued without a hitch. The program was a list of celebrities. The finest singers in the world were realizing the Wagnerian drama. Caruso played Siegfried, and we were in the depths of the delight into which his power and timbre had plunged us when the bird sang.[1]

You will recall that there is in *Siegfried* a singing bird—which is to say, a woman, in the wings, who lends the bird the prestige of words and melody. Thus, an invisible woman suddenly began to sing—and then it seemed to us that all the other singers had merely been mewling, roaring or braying since the curtain went up. The sonorous sounds of the impeccable orchestra immediately became screechy and annoying, so magical was that voice. Its purity was only equaled by its strength. It combined all the virtues that sounds can acquire, and did so in a manner so incomparable, unprecedented and superhuman, that everyone wondered, at first, whether a human throat was really emitting that prodigious song, or whether it might be some strange independent voice with a life of its own . . .

But on listening to it, no, no: that caressant soprano revealed a feminine soul, the ardent heart of a young woman who was breathing it out in a charmingly natural fashion, as a flower yields its perfume . . .

On listening to it, one divined as its source a vermilion mouth and palpitating white breasts . . .

One shivered, on listening to it, as if gazing at the freshness of an excessively beautiful virgin . . .

---

1 Enrico Caruso (1873-1921) was world famous by the time this story was published, but in the 1890s, when it is set, he was still singing in provincial Italian theaters; he did not make it to La Scala until 1900 and his recording career did not begin until 1902.

Who, then, was singing in that fashion? My memory recalled, one by one, the voices of the world's most famous singers. I knew them all. I thought for a moment that one of them had taken us by surprise by accepting that minor role—but no prima donna could have rivaled, in voice or skill, the fay who was singing the bird in the wings.

She fell silent. There was a sensational rustle in the audience. The program was consulted. It bore only one name that was obscure, which every eye sought out: *Borelli.*

The public awaited with bizarre impatience the bird's next entrance in the scene and the moment when the unknown woman would begin to sing again. For my part, I was subject to a tyrannical desire to hear her voice . . .

It finally sprang forth, and streamed over us like a subtle and bewitching wave, in which one could have wished to bathe forever . . .

When La Borelli stopped singing for the second and last time that evening, the crowd must have suffered a chagrin akin to pain, for a great dolorous sigh was heard to swell, from the stalls to the highest boxes. Then the applause burst forth, so impetuous that the orchestra stopped playing. The standing spectators clapped their hands, demanding that the diva appear and take a bow. It was in vain, however, that Caruso extended an inviting arm toward the wings; Mademoiselle—or Madame—Borelli refused, presumably unwilling to exhibit her pretty face in the stage-lights without make-up.

I took advantage of the mundane tumult to slip away to the wings in order to discover the phenomenon. Gunsbourg, the director, intercepted me. He was radiant.

"What a revelation, eh, my dear chap!"

"But who is she? Borelli, Borelli . . . a pseudonym? It's miraculous, the voice of a maiden with the experience of a seasoned artiste! Amazing! What authority! What warmth! What . . ."

"What a revelation, eh!"

Gunsbourg could not get over it. As for me, I had but one idea: to engage La Borelli at the Opéra-Dramatique—and I admit that frankly. But Gunsbourg shook his head mockingly. "That, you know, is something else!"

I assumed that he had contracted with the singer for a long series of performances. He corrected my misapprehension, but swore nevertheless—still in a bantering tone—that Madame Borelli would never appear on the stage of my theater.

"Is it that she doesn't know how to act?" I asked. "Bah! She'll learn. It's a mere detail. Her diction already leaves nothing to be desired. Introduce me to her, my dear chap—quickly. I'll take responsibility for the rest."

"Hold on! She's already leaving! There she is at the end of the corridor with her husband. Well, are you coming?"

A couple had just emerged into the corridor through a side-door and, having turned their backs toward us, were drawing away. I glimpsed them for a few seconds before they reached the far corner: he, an imposing stature enveloped in dark clothing; she, a meager imprecise form propped up on two crutches that made her shoulders rise and fall rhythmically and dug into her armpits at every tottering step.

The unparalleled cantatrice was a cripple!

I felt a cruel disappointment, the violence of which astonished me when I recovered from my stupor.

The Borellis were on their way out. Gunsbourg was waiting.

"What does it matter!" I eventually exclaimed, in the ardor of my enthusiasm. "There's no lameness that can hold her back! After they've heard her sing, every composer will want her as an interpreter. They'll write roles to suit her, episodic, motionless or hidden—roles of admirable originality! Roles for voices, not for characters! What do I know? Then again, we have the resource of concerts—in that respect, the field is wide open. In any case, my dear chap, it's *essential* that she be heard. Think of it! Centuries might pass before such a vocal prodigy is reproduced—if it ever is reproduced! I'm astonished that your company-member isn't famous in spite of her infirmity. Where the Devil did you unearth that nightingale?"

"I saw her for the first time a week ago. She arrived in my office one evening, escorted by her husband, or at least by an individual who claimed to be her husband. He's a rather disquieting character, shady in appearance and manner. Both of them, decked out in unspeakable rags, seemed to be very poor. Their bearing, however, respired the health of vagabonds accustomed to the open air. I thought they'd come from Italy, perhaps as beggars . . . but in sum, no one knows where they come from. Monsieur Borelli argued the conditions of the engagement with revolting rudeness. He has his hooks into his companion, that's obvious. She has that constrained physiognomy of Lakmés or Mignons,[1] and surely wouldn't sing unless someone were forcing her to do it. Poor girl! Did you notice the melancholy quality of her voice?"

No, I hadn't noticed that. Besides, my project was preoccupying my mind.

"Give me their address," I said, brusquely. "I must take that woman to Paris."

The Bohemians' household occupied two small rooms in a fourth-rate hotel called the Villa des Mouettes, over-looking the sea. It happened that I was staying nearby. I went there the next day, early in the morning.

Without the least protocol, a boy led me to their apartment. "They're on the first floor," he told me, "be-cause of the lady's incapacity. There's no lift here, and no rooms on the ground floor." As the blast of a trumpet shook the whole the building, he added: "He's the one playing the hunting-horn. He's already been told three times to shut up."

---

1 *Lakmé* (1883) and *Mignon* (1866) are both light operas. The former has words by Edmond Gondinet and Philippe Gille and music by Léo Delibes; it is based on a work by Pierre Loti and set in India; the latter has words by Michel Carré and Jules Barbier, inspired by Goethe (Mignon is a character in *Wilhelm Meister*) and music by Ambroise Thomas.

We arrived in front of a door that the interior fan-fare—savage and scandalous, but not without a certain crude beauty—was causing to vibrate.

My guide knocked. Silence fell abruptly. I perceived a muffled dialogue, the sound of something moving away, being dragged across the carpet, the closing of a door, then the opening of a window . . . the click-click of a key . . .

Finally, Borelli appeared.

Face to face, we recoiled. For my part, it was surprise, at the sight of that astonishingly chubby, suntanned, curly-haired gallows-bird—a sort of dangerous Hercules, half-dressed in trousers and a loose jacket, and who . . . in truth, I don't know how to express it . . .

I had a vague sensation of having met that man somewhere before—and recently, damn it!—but *in circumstances such that I should never have seen him again.* Do you see? The fact of seeing him again seemed—obscurely—impossible. It was a vague impression—so vague that a moment's reasoning immediately attributed it to the remembrance of some dream.

Borelli's suspicion was not so quick to dissipate. Anxiety widened his eyes, and I didn't understand the reason for it—for, far from explaining my reminiscence, my host's attitude seemed to contradict it. I had a muted consciousness of that relationship.

I bowed. Borelli's face lit up.

"Damn!" he said, blowing into his abnormal cheeks. "You frightened me, with your big white beard! *Perbacco, signore*—you should warn people, when you resemble someone else so closely!"

I offered him my card. He burst into loud laughter, from which I inferred that he could not read. That is why I told him my name and my position. Then he invited me to sit down.

I explained the purpose of my visit, neglecting to mention crutches and lameness, while surreptitiously taking inventory of the lodgings. Borelli, impelled by false modesty, had hidden his hunting-horn. I was only able to discover miserable impersonal furniture: two chairs; an iron-framed bed; a chest of drawers; a cheapjack clock flanked by two large spiny seashells on the mantelpiece; lithographs and coat-pegs on the walls; and the most wretched trunk imaginable—moldy and falling apart—in a corner, like debris washed ashore after a shipwreck.

Confronted by that indigence, pity gradually softened my attitude. My offers reflected that. They were . . . what they needed to be.

Borelli listened to them without saying a word. He gazed through the open window at the sea, with piercing eyes. The toes of his bare, sun-bronzed feet played with their sandals. In the opening of his jacket, the brown torso of a Neapolitan athlete could be seen swelling with the rhythm of life. Oh, what a handsome fellow! But where had I seen him before?

Furrowing his brows and clenching his fists, he muttered: "Just my luck!" And he began laughing sarcastically. "I knew I'd be offered loads of gold and silver," he went on. "Just my luck! *I can't, perbacco!* We *can't* accept. We can't go to Paris, you see, Monsieur Director. I'm obliged to refuse. Oh, existence on land isn't easy! I even wonder if we'll succeed in living here . . . you know, don't you, that Madame Borelli is a cripple?"

"I don't care about that. No one will care about it. She sings, and one is all ears. She sings, and one no longer has eyes . . ."

"Isn't that so? Isn't it? You've never heard singing like that, eh? Can you believe that she has such treasures in her throat? Oh, tell me, anyway—do you think I could make a lot of money with her? What would you say to concerts in the dark? Darkness and music—they go together. No one ever sees her . . . then again, it would economize on lighting. What do you think? Tell me, Monsieur Director? I'm thinking about a tour along the coast: Nice, Marseilles . . ."

Profoundly sickened by the manners of this boor, who spoke of his wife and a great artiste as a curious object, I nevertheless replied: "But why don't you want to try Paris? I guarantee . . ."

The enormous lout cut me off, curtly. "Basta! Basta! I said the coast; it will be the coast! We only do seaside resorts. It's for health reasons, Madame's whim, family secrets—anything you want, but *that's—the—way—it—is!* The coast or nothing."

He had the same effect on me as a rare wild beast. My opinion was further reinforced when Borelli, having distinguished the splashing sound of ablutions in the next room—which, moreover, must have splashed the surroundings copiously—ran to the connecting door, opened it by a crack, and cursed the author of the splashing in singularly barbarous terms. He was terrible in his fury and vehemence.

There was no response, but Madame Borelli—at least, I assume that it was her—continued taking her bath in a more subdued fashion.

The other, mollified, returned to me. "I regret it, damn it! I regret it, *perbacco*!—for the wages, as is reasonable . . . and also . . . you seem like a nice old fellow. We'd be fixed up . . ."

He looked me up and down with disdainful benevolence.

"I'm at your disposal," I replied, politely.

The bumpkin misunderstood the conventional meaning of the formula. "Really?" he said. "Really and truly?" Drawing closer, he looked me in the eye without restraint. "Really, truly and honestly?"

The sad lot of the singer moved me to such pity that I made a sign of acquiescence with my eyes and head.

With that, Borelli said to me in a low voice: "Well then listen: you can do me a big favor."

"Go on."

"If you . . ." He stared at me severely, then, satisfied with my attitude, resumed in a confidential mode, perhaps a trifle hesitantly: "If you see a man hereabouts *who resembles you like your mirror image*, tell me right away."

I pretended to accept the mission. "A man with a long white beard? Very old?"

"Rather!" said Borelli, with a bitterly ironic smile.

"How is he dressed?"

He seemed perplexed. "Dressed? In faith . . . not very fashionably, doubtless. Baroque, probably. Ah! There's this: try to get a look at his forehead. His forehead ought to bear the mark of a . . . an overly heavy hat, worn for a long time. Just now, when you appeared, that's how I knew you weren't him . . . but it's the beard, most of all, that you'll pick out."

"What if he's shaved?"

My interlocutor smiled again, this time without bitterness. The thought of my mysterious double stripped of his beard seemed to fill him with delight. "Have no fear, Monsieur Director. There are beards one does not shave off. And thanks, you know—he is, so to speak, a creditor . . . who's tracking me . . ."

He looked at the sea, thoughtfully.

In order to prolong the conversation and, if possible, get more deeply into the confidence of the enigmatic churl, I ventured: "I can see that you love the sea."

He emerged from his reverie, and his reddened cheeks puffed out. "Me? The sea?" he gasped. "Ugh . . . why ask me that? No, I don't love the sea. It stinks, doesn't it? You can smell the tide. Don't you think that you can smell the fish even from here? No? That's not what you were trying to insinuate? No? I can!" He raised his voice abruptly, in a menacing fashion: "I can! It smells of fish here!"

His keen eyes sparkled, fixed on mine. I thought I ought to withdraw without further ado, and took my leave of the irritable nomad, asking him to convey to Madame Borelli the assurance of my utter admiration and the regret I bore for not having been able to offer my homage to her.

"She's getting dressed," Borelli countered.

I was not yet outside when the fanfare thundered more loudly than before.

The Hercules with the pygian cheeks had closed his window—but I perceived, at the next one, the desperate face of a woman who was gazing at the sea and weeping.

✳

I saw the Borellis again that same evening, at the theater and in the wings. A veritable multitude was crowding the auditorium to heard *Siegfried*'s bird sing. Our Parisian party had remained in Monte Carlo in its entirety, contrary to the plans we had made to return to Paris the day after the performance. The previous night's audience had returned in full, replete with melomaniac fervor. For lack of a smaller folding-seat, Gunsbourg had offered me a stool behind one of the scenery-supports. It was the best way of getting close to Madame Borelli. I watched out for her.

They arrived. The most lamentable of all the memories I have is that of the invalid advancing jerkily on her crutches in the midst of other actors magnificent in their carriage and radiant with pride. The unfortunate woman was clad in poverty-stricken Sunday clothes. I shall long remember her shapeless and colorless bonnet, undoubtedly the victim of many a downpour, diabolically positioned, but on a superb chignon whose fawn-colored tresses were tightly wound, compressing their fabulous opulence. And her bodice! The poor woman! How many times had she laundered that smock to get it into that urine-colored state? And her skirt! Her pitiful skirt, with its faded hues, superannuated petticoats, "decorated" with garlands and worn braid—her sinister skirt, knotted at the base like a sack, upon the secret monstrosity of her legs!

She moved heavily, positioning the sack, then the crutches, then the sack . . .

I couldn't tell you whether she was pretty; one only saw her sadness. She looked as if she had been born on the Day of the Dead.

Monsieur Borelli held her close. I perceived a vague similarity between them, like a family resemblance, a certain wild, russet, suntanned quality that linked them confusedly together. Brother and sister? Cousins? Or simply compatriots?

On seeing me, the man stopped short. He resumed walking immediately, his expression reassured and his cheeks puffed out.

"It's a bit strong! I can't get used to your beard!" he said to me, as he shook my hand. Then, very quickly, he whispered in my ear: "No news? The old man? Good." He straightened up again. "This is my wife, Monsieur Director."

I tried to get the cantatrice to talk. She murmured a few *yesses* and a few discouraging *noes* . . . besides, the performance was under way; we didn't have the right to talk. The music reigned.

Siegfried's horn resounded. Borelli gripped my shoulder and whispered; "Isn't that beautiful? Isn't that trumpet beautiful? That's what I call a nice piece, easy to remember . . ."

Suddenly, the voice of the bird emerged from the lips of the invalid, so close to me that my throat resonated with it. It was as if the atmosphere were saturated with a maddening sonorous aroma. Seized by vertigo, intoxication, gratitude, I became unsteady on my feet. Scene-shifters, chorus girls, bit-part players and even singers—the entire personnel of the theater—formed a circle around the cripple. There was something in her voice other than genius and sweetness; there was an inexplicable power of attraction. And in the half-light of the place, magnified, transfigured by the love of her art, the golden-haired cripple acquired an irresistible beauty . . .

She finished. The continuing opera was a tiresome racket. I emerged from an opium dream. La Borelli was no longer anything more than a sad and badly-dressed creature, who could not be cheered up by my praises. The ovations left her indifferent. Her escort led her away hurriedly—"to avoid indiscretions at the exit," he said. I wanted to go with them; he refused, with an ill grace.

An hour later, unable to calm the agitation that the emotion, though brief, had left within me, I was wandering along the edge of the sea, some distance away from the houses. The silhouette of a man standing on a rock was suddenly outlined in the darkness.

The new moon illuminated the marine landscape faintly. I thought I recognized Borelli. Divided between dread and curiosity, I advanced furtively through the boulders on the shore, continually losing sight of him only to discover him closer at hand, as motionless as his pedestal. It was definitely him, like a statue.

Where had I met him before?

Remembering the scares that the unexpected sight of me gave him, I paused some distance away and announced myself joyfully. He shivered nonetheless upon his rock, like a cypress in a gust of wind.

Borelli seemed to be lost in contemplation before the nocturnal sea. A large cloak draped him in Romanticism. Diffuse objects were heaped at his feet.

"You can't tell me that you don't love Amphitrite!" I exclaimed, in a bantering tone. "To come at this hour to admire her . . ."

"So what?" he grunted. "Is it any of your business? Yes, I love the sea, but not so much as solitude, you know!"

I was astonished to hear him speaking so loudly, in a voice that overwhelmed the sound of the waves, when I was so close to him. I felt his anger. He said to me, point-blank: "Why don't you dare to interrogate me about what's on the ground beside me?"

"But I hadn't even given it a thought. . . ." I replied, disconcerted.

Borelli shrugged his shoulders. I observed that his eyes were uniquely occupied with the sea. He studied its moving expanse unrelentingly. It was quiet and pallid in the moonlight. A dolphin was playing in the waves; its contortions and the flips of its tail were visible from time to time in fugitive gleams. The lighthouses, all in a line, gesticulated variously with their infinite arms of light.

"You haven't given it a thought?" he mocked. "Go on! You're scared. I hate intruders—you know that very well. Leave me in peace, my dear Monsieur!"

I was only an old man, devoid of vigor . . .

"Listen, Borelli—I'm going, that's understood. It's far from my intention to be disagreeable to you, my lad. But don't say that I'm scared. I'm not scared. What are those things at your feet?"

"Go away!" bellowed the colossus. "Peace! Peace! Peace! If not . . ."

I beat the retreat at a steady pace, mastering a furious desire to run away as fast as my legs could carry me.

As I went back into Monte Carlo, I wondered if it might be wise to take advantage of the absence of the redoubtable cicisbeo to attempt to have a conversation with Madame Borelli. The lateness of the hour held me back. Both the adventurers' windows were dark; the invalid's slumber seemed to be a delight that should only be broken in exchange for another. I passed on.

The adventure seemed supremely exciting to me; a voice captivated me; a woman excited my charity; a man intrigued my suspicion. I allowed my traveling companions to leave without me.

In the early afternoon, Borelli had himself announced. I received him in my room. It was a social visit, or so he claimed. No allusion was made to the previous night's incident. After a few superfluous remarks, though, he asked me straight out to lend him twenty-five louis.

Very annoyed, I procrastinated, changing the subject; I offered him my compliments with regard to the affluence that the singer was attracting to the theater and the principality. Thanks to her, the accommodation was fully booked for a fortnight and the hotels were overflowing.

On that, the husband-impresario told me that he was going to demand a serious pay-increase from Gunsbourg, or his wife would not sing again. I assume that he was on the point of reiterating his request for five hundred francs, but an unexpected occurrence interrupted him.

His face changed. With his ear cocked, he gestured to me to be silent. Before I had heard whatever it was, the fanatic hurled himself on to the balcony.

All the passers-by and strollers were heading in the same direction at a hurried pace, with a hypnotic and taciturn gait that was alarming at first glance. In the distance, in the direction of the Villa des Mouettes, an extraordinary voice launched forth in disorganized song—and it was toward that voice that all those people were marching like sleep-walkers.

My visitor lost his temper. "I've forbidden her, though . . ."

What happened next was immediate. Four bounds had taken him to the foot of the staircase, as he too hastened toward the magnetic singer.

Was it the effect of the indomitable curiosity that linked me to their destiny? Was it by virtue of the melodious magnetism? At any rate, the fact is that I bounded after him.

From every direction, people were running toward the barbed call of the voice. What she was singing resembled nothing familiar. It sprang forth, twisting and overflowing in delightful cries. It was the entirety of springtime, singing the entirety of love. Men, sub-jugated, were heading toward the infernal canticle as little birds head toward the eyes of a serpent. There were some women trying to hold some of them back, and others who were following them toward the voice. Arms extended, eyes crazed, their feverish legs were working mechanically. A host of fanatical automata was pressing at the doorway of the Villa des Mouettes and beneath the singer's open window. Borelli threw himself into it with a forceful leap, waving his arms and legs, progress-ing with great thrusts of the hips and shoulders into the bosom of that living wave, with the gestures and a swimmer and an amphibious flexibility. The ecstatic members of the crowd allowed themselves to be brutal-ized. They were listening, with their mouths open and their nostrils flared, as if their mouths and nostrils were listening, drinking and breathing in the voice, obedient to its despotic tones: *Closer! Closer! Forward!* That was what was being ordered without being spoken.

Like everyone else, I was held voluptuously captive by the toils of the melody, and I immersed myself invol-untarily in the human heap in order to get closer, at any price, my eardrums fascinated, my soul numbed . . .

It was resonating in the depths of a gulf, into which all those amorous individuals wanted to precipitate themselves.

The charm lasted until the intervention of the plump manager. His outburst reached us as a fearful summons, proffered in an idiom that was impossible to compre-hend . . .

Then, crushed by a silence more silent than any other, we looked at one another as if emerging from an adorable and shameful dementia. Everyone resumed his interrupted journey, head empty, nerves jangling, full of astonishment and confusion. Many had glided as far as the threshold of the room; they slipped away, blushing. A few were weeping. Life recommenced; the noises of it set all their teeth on edge.

That kind of scandal only had fortunate consequences for my friend Gunsbourg. Madame Borelli sang the bird as she had the night before, in the presence of an elite audience which crammed the corridors and blocked the exits, a noisy and profuse crush; but Wagner's music on her lips was not sufficiently imperious a spell to draw the legion of her admirers into the wings.

I was placed in the orchestra stalls.

On raising my eyes, I perceived in the balcony, directly above my head, an old gentleman whose long white beard made me shiver. The opera-glasses revealed the image that mirrors habitually relay back to me, with the difference that, of the two of us, it was me that was the reflection. I was the faded, soft and discolored replica of that august old man; the copy of which he was the original. With the complexion of an old sea-dog, a Roman nose, two turquoise flames beneath shadowy eyebrows, and his forehead barred by a reddish line like those left by heavy helmets, he looked like the venerable admiral of a squadron of yore, a commander grown old in naval glory, a doge of Venice, mistress of the sea, immortal or resurrected. A frock-coat constrained the amplitude of his torso. Many a lady was peering at that combined patriarchal and military majesty through her opera-glasses. Royal names were running from mouth to mouth in his respect.

There was no doubt about it: this was Signor Borelli's enemy—perhaps even his ancestor and the ancestor of the singer; for, it must be admitted, the family resemblance I had already noted assimilated all three of their faces.

That of the old man took on an expression of tragic grandeur when the bird began to sing. Its ancient solemn rectitude shifted nervously, as if to deplore . . .

Bravos. Encores. Hurrahs. Disorder.

I tried to find him again. He had disappeared.

Ought I to warn the interested party? I hesitated over that until the final act and concluded by opting in favor of the old man, against the persecutor of my protégée. Borelli's adversary could only be a friend of the oppressed woman, an ally for me; it was, therefore, her and not the Italian who had to be informed as soon as possible.

In the hope that the plump man would devote himself once again to the shadowy task in which I had disturbed him on the strand on the previous night, and which, no doubt, would prevent him from leaving the shore, I went to the Mouettes.

The drowsy concierge mumbled that neither Monsieur nor Madame Borelli had come back from the theater—to which he swore—and that, moreover, they never came back before three or four o'clock in the morning, *which he had already told me a little while ago*, and that he did not understand why I had woken him up twice in succession to ask him the same thing.

The news of that double absence confused my ideas and upset my plan. Moreover, *the old man had been there*. I resolved to bring the matter into the light, and set off resolutely for the rocks where Borelli had snapped at me. Having had second thoughts, though, I turned back; I climbed to the top of the cliff that bordered that part of the shore, from whose heights I would be able to look down on the setting and the action.

My heart was beating rapidly. I felt strange.

The nebulous night was not as favorable to watchers as the one before, and the moon was still on the point of rising. The sea—the ancient sea, the Latin sea—lulling its eternal insomnia, was reciting its pagan legends and the poem of its mythology in the darkness. Flecks of foam whitened it here and there. Clouds being sparse, the clarity of the sky showed me the fugitive gleams of the nautical play of a dolphin in the far distance. But then the thunderous clamor of a horn went up—a horn sounding Siegfried's fanfare!

I stopped.

Beneath my post, there was a statue standing on a pedestal: Borelli, who was sounding the trumpet-call on an instrument so small that it could not be seen; Borelli *alone*; a sculptural Borelli.

Ah! I thought, suddenly. God, how stupid I am! I didn't realize it until now. He doesn't resemble any *actual* citizen! It's the Tritons he resembles, with his bloated cheeks! The Tritons of painters and sculptors! The two decorative Tritons of the water-pavilion at the Palais de Longchamp, in Marseilles, at which I was looking only the other day! All well and good! That's why it seemed impossible to encounter him, since he wasn't in the land of dreams!"

The fanfare having concluded, Borelli called out to someone—but he was still alone. I was looking at him from behind. He was standing between the sea and me, on the rock, in his overcoat. His calls multiplied, and became more precipitate, to the point at which he seemed to be hurling invective at the waves. He really was calling out, but to whom? Darkness. No one.

He crouched down, and leapt down from the rock. He was no longer visible . . .

Oh! Yes: at the very edge, on the fringe of the waves.

And the horn began to sound again—no longer Siegfried's leitmotiv but long howls reminiscent of what hunting jargon terms a *compulsory summons*. And then again, another bitter discourse shouted in the solitude, into the Mediterranean darkness: the liquid desert where a single dolphin was frolicking. And then the insistent trumpet call again, imperative, roaring . . .

Nothing more.

The moon was veiled with cloud.

Borelli was dragging something out of the sea— something that resisted him. Like a fisherman hauling in his net—the simulacrum of a fisherman hauling in his net, of which absolutely nothing could be seen. Ah! The thing had yielded, had broken; having fallen backwards, he blasphemed. I heard foreign words, imprecations . . .

He was struggling on the spot. Suddenly, I saw that he was naked. In the same instant, he slid sinuously into the water, swimming with the rapidity of a seal, with great thrusts of his shoulders and hips, just as he had surged through the middle of the crowd . . .

Fascination, equal to a passion, made me tremble. The most fantastic thing of all, however, had not yet occurred.

While the Hercules was swimming out into the open sea, becoming blurred in the depths of the darkness—heading almost directly for the dolphin, which could no longer be made out—I heard a kind of whinnying sound, *out at sea*. Several others followed, mingling together; gigantic, paradoxical whinnying sounds, with an unusual resonance; a choir of stallions imitating the barking concert of seals; horses crossed with walruses; ambiguous striders of the shadows and the sea . . .

At that moment, another of Borelli's calls reached me, above the din.

An infinitely distant voice answered him . . .

I just had time to throw myself flat on the ground and stick my fingers in my ears. I had just felt myself marching forward, toward the edge of the cliff. One more step, and I would have been dead. For that faraway voice, from the remotest distance, was the hallucinatory voice of Madame Borelli, frenzied now, and triumphant, who was singing her springtime song like a hymn of deliverance!

Slowly, I relaxed the vice-like grip of my fists upon my ears; by that means I established that the human voice and the whinnyings had vanished.

The moon emerged from a mass of cloud.

In the sea, a moving dot was heading straight for the shore; another dot, gleaming was following it a few fathoms behind: two men. The first came ashore. That was Borelli again. Dripping and panting, he headed for Monte Carlo. The second stood up at the same spot, and immediately launched himself on the heels of the fugitive. That one was an old man, and he was a giant— the old man whose feeble miniature I was. His long white beard floated in the wind of the pursuit. A golden crown helmeted him with spikes and fire. Although devoid of clothes, he would have been reminiscent of Charlemagne had he not been more sovereign than any emperor. At the end of one superb and menacing arm he was brandishing a sort of fork, like a lance and like a scepter.

The pursuit disappeared into the unknown.

I remained alone with the immensity.

After an hour of waiting in the moonlight, I decided to leave the theater of that equivocal drama. Before doing anything else, however, I went down a path to the place that Borelli had haunted for two nights in a row, to my knowledge—and every night, in my belief.

I found his felt hat there and his Romantic cloak. Next to them, on a parcel of old clothes, easily recognizable as Madame Borelli's, were two crutches forming a cross. There was also a large spiny seashell on the cloak: a conch.

By virtue of searching for the place where I had glimpsed the nocturnal wanderer trying to haul in the thing whose rupture had made him fall over, I ended up discovering a stake solidly planted in the sand, on the tide-line. It still retained a fine and resilient steel cord, which plunged into the sea. I pulled out about two hundred meters—all of it. It ended in a large collar, or rather a girdle—a leather girdle with a padlock, which had been cut a little while before.

As for Borelli, his body was blocking the path half way to Monte Carlo. He was lying face down, facing Monaco. Death, aided by the moonlight, was whitening his colossal back to the point of giving it a green tinge. Three parallel wounds, equidistant and in the same line, offered evidence of a single thrust of an avenging trident.

# THE SONG OF THE SIRENS

## by Renée Vivien

### I

"I should like," said Ione with the violet eyes, lingering on the crepuscular shore, "to hear the Song of the Sirens."

"You know very well," replied the old fisherman Meniskos, "that the Song of the Sirens is mortal to those who hear it."

"Like everything that is beautiful and sonorous," the virgin with the violet eyes interjected, imperiously. "Only things without grandeur contain no danger."

"The sage Ulysses gave his companions the advice to block their ears with wax and attach themselves to the masts of the vessel," added Meniskos.

"Ulysses was nothing but a coward," cried the very young and very imperious Ione. "And his companions were also nothing but cowards. Prudence is eternal cowardice. Oh, to prefer the tedious Penelope to the Sirens! Myself, I would give the breath of my lips, the line, undulations and colors that my avid eyes contemplate with so much anguish, the harmonies that make me suffer so divinely, the perfumes that I respire with so much fever, everything that makes life burning and sad, to hear the Song of the Sirens for an instant . . . And the kisses of my companions, the kisses that are like harmonies, perfumes, the joy of colors, lines and graceful undulations, the kisses as bitter as the sky and as sweet as roses, I would give them all to hear the perilous Song for an instant."

"In truth, your words are not wise," said old Meniskos, calmly. "What! You would give the long years of a human existence for a lightning flash of joy?"

"You cannot understand, Meniskos," Ione replied. "Men are cowards from birth. Only two instincts make them act: pride and bestiality. No man would ever give his existence to hear the Song of the Sirens."

Meniskos shrugged his shoulders, and went away, toward the hearth and the evening meal. In the twilight, Ione detached the boat, which was lost in the mist in which Visions floated.

She wandered for three days and three nights. And the Sirens appeared to her, in a green moonlight that broke over the waves . . .

Their song was as imprecise as the song of the waves; it attracted like the mysterious appeal of the waves; it unfurled with a grave amplitude, like the sob of the Ocean; it gripped the soul of Ione, who sank voluptuously into the waves . . .

# II

She awoke, the drowned child with the violet eyes, under the fluid kisses of a Siren whose hair enveloped her like networks of algae. She awoke under the ungraspable gaze of green eyes, which had the perfidious softness of the waves. She awoke under the troubled smile of the Siren, whose voice, like the distant sound of waves on crepuscular shores, said to her:

"Since you have loved us resolutely enough to give us your human existence, we will give you in our turn the fervor of our kiss. See, I have collected with my own hands, in order to ornament your hair, the pearls that are the pale flowers of the Sea, and multicolored nacre, and the infinite grace of marvelous seashells. Your repose on the velvet of the silver sand will be lulled by the rhythm of the Sea. You will play with the crabs and you will smile at the medusae that burn like the stars. In the gardens of the Sea, living anemones are blue, and in her orchards, trees of coral sway their red branches at the whim of the eddies. You will hear the Sea's song of eternally unappeased amour, the song that rises toward the Moon, her distant Lover. For Death cures all memories, and Death is very beautiful on the bed of the Sea.

# MR. CUFFYCOAT'S CURIOUS ADVENTURE

## by André Lichtenberger

O N SUNDAY the twenty-eighth of June 1914, as was his habit, Mr. Cuffycoat, having informed his housekeeper that he would be dining at his club, slipped into his smoking-jacket and, before going out, studied himself one last time in his wardrobe mirror.

The sight of his round face, his colorful cheeks, his blue, slightly protruding eyes and his entire solid and upright person had not been a surprise to him for quite a long time. It never failed to procure him a comfortable sensation—comfortable rather than esthetic, strictly speaking. The age of fifty had softened his features and marked his flesh with red blotches. Two warts, one of which bore a spiky tuft of hair, were tending toward a ridiculous enlargement. One of his incisors, recently chipped, caused an asymmetrical gap in his jaw, which irritated him. He noticed, moreover, that his shirt, poorly ironed, had a crease, and would have to be changed, even at the inconvenience of undressing. As for the smoking-jacket, although he was not a slave to any excessive snobbery, it would surely be opportune to replace it in the autumn. He similarly postponed a visit to the dentist until the same epoch.

All things considered, he was no more displeasing than the average gentleman of his age in possession of an annual income between a thousand and fifteen hundred pounds and living in South Kensington. One might even say that he resembled the majority of them in an incontestable fashion. As everyone knows, fauna adapt to the conditions of the environment in which they live. The chameleon takes on the color of the foliage that shelters it, and the neck of the giraffe is elongated exactly as much as is required to browse the fresh shoots of tall trees. Mr. Cuffycoat presented a completely satisfactory specimen of the human variety that, in the bosom of family hotels, taxis and tube trains, has ended up distinguishing itself in several notable characteristics from cave-dwellers.

To tell the truth, though, it was not exactly his physical personality that Mr. Cuffycoat was weighing up, as a disciple of Phidias or George Brummell might have done. Even though Jemima Barnet, and several other young women having today attained a rich maturity, would once gladly have placed their delicate hand in his for life, he obtained no vanity from that. That was merely the cupboard, the correctly-fashioned chest of drawers, no more, in which a soul dwelt.

Or, rather than a soul—there are too many thorny misapprehensions attached to the meaning of that term—I propose to say to you: a spiritual essence. And there again, at the risk of prolonging this introduction, I am obliged to persist. It would be inexact to think that

Mr. Cuffycoat disposed of intellectual gifts or moral quantities of an extreme refinement. You might have consulted the list of his social and philosophical works at the British Museum, and even opened some of them. They do not surpass in any way the average of those sold at Tooth & Sons. As for the delicacy of his conscience, I am convinced that if he refused the preference shares that he was offered by that rogue Percy Lyon for the launch of Vaseline Mines, it was less because it was fraudulent than because the fraud in question seemed to him to be too gross not to end in criminal proceedings.

All that, I am aware, does not sufficiently distinguish Mr. Cuffycoat from many other gentlemen who frequent the second-rate restaurants of Piccadilly, and I would not have thought of making him the hero of this tale if he had not imposed himself on public attention by a more characteristic shibboleth.

It is appropriate—I have no doubt that you will agree with me—to credit everyone with the gifts that belong to him. It is an absurd pettiness to contest them. I would never deny that Lady Nashburn has asthma, the third-ranked pearl necklace in the realm and very solid religious principles. Mr. Doomberry—James Doomberry, the one who lives in Montpensier Street—is an exceptional conchyliologist. Among all the regulars at Turtle's Bar, Jack Hitchpin is the foremost in deciphering the puzzles in the weekly papers and David Robertson in the game of draughts.

Mr. Cuffycoat's specialty is of a much higher order. You are not unaware of the degree to which many people—distinguished minds such as Marcus Aurelius,

Pascal, William James, John Stuart Mill and many others—have been haunted by all the philosophical, sociological and political problems that never cease to occupy the most prominent place, after the advertisements, in the columns of the newspapers. Hence, endless discussions, enormous volumes, headaches, troubled digestions. Mr. Cuffycoat has had the rare merit of cutting short all those divagations on that dangerous terrain.

Of that ensemble of questions he has made two categories. There are those that can only preoccupy neurasthenics. Those, as they emerge from Cambridge, he has locked in a drawer, throwing the key into the Thames from the middle of London Bridge. That way, he is sure of no longer hearing any mention of them. Then there are those that it is appropriate for a gentleman in Mr. Cuffycoat's position to talk about at a dinner party or in the pages of the *Athenaeum*. With regard to those, Mr. Cuffycoat has the good fortune to possess the truth. In the same epoch, armed with a hook, he has carefully made his choice from all the stock that his masters had accumulated in him during his schooldays, and having eliminated everything that was not of the finest quality, he has verified, weighed, labeled and catalogued all the rest, and has arranged them admirably within the cupboard or chest of drawers that his mirror presents to him when he looks into it. He can give his word, as a gentleman, that he has undertaken that operation with minute care; thus, all the scoria, all the false semblances and all the dubious items having been set aside, he has at the disposal of his contemporaries the complete arsenal of Truths desirable in a well-made intelligence.

Although the list is not as long as you might think, I shall not try to enumerate its items for you, but I shall give you the Ariadne's thread that will permit you to navigate through the furniture, if you are curious to do so.

In substance, this is the nub: Providence—a pseudonym whose secret is in the drawer whose key has been lost at London Bridge—has arranged everything in this world for the happiness of humankind. Undoubtedly, there have been a few misunderstandings between them, the importance of which universal history has grossly magnified. They have been diminishing incessantly, and, for two centuries, it has been possible to affirm that everything is settled to a remarkable degree. In the last fifty years, particularly, the pace of progress has been so vertiginous that it has been able to surprise minds less alert than Mr. Cuffycoat's. Having the good fortune to possess the Truth, however, he has recorded all of that as a perfectly normal receipt.

Science, by means of its new discoveries, incessantly augments the means of human enjoyment, and brings about a parallel amelioration. A host of statistics offers peremptory proof of the daily increase in its conquests; look at those concerning potatoes, pigs and longevity. Those that have the appearance of contradicting the others—the increases in alcoholism, criminality, etc.—are of absolutely no significance, as I could easily demonstrate to you if we had the time. The Truth—with a capital T—that Mr. Cuffycoat has solidly installed in his cupboard is that within every State, increasingly fortunate citizens are entering into increasingly satisfactory relations, and in the same way, States are in the process of substituting for the anarchic rivalries of old the pacific settlement of their disputes, while waiting for humankind as a whole to form a single reconciled family in which the entire world will eat breakfast, play football, do a little work, constitute stocks and embrace one another at the same times of day.

It is a great fortune for a nation to possess citizens like Mr. Cuffycoat. It is necessary to recognize that the deposits of wisdom that he contains are not yet as extensively exploited as the coal-mines of Yorkshire or American oil-wells, but already, its rich alluvia are flowing through the liberal and conservative press and between the lips of Statesmen. It will not take long for the entire country to satisfy its spiritual needs therewith as generally as it butters its toast and takes a bath.

If it were reasonable to attach himself to such futile impressions, Mr. Cuffycoat, in the radiant peace of the summer evening, would experience a surfeit of satisfaction in possessing such vast reserves of Truth to provision all the clientele that comes knocking at the door of the cupboard. A master trader, he only draws for his security a more kindly indulgence for the enervation that is manifest, on his arrival in the smoking-room, by Phil Norwood and Jack Clinton, who are mixing their whisky with a dose of the evening newspapers. It appears that some sort of Archduke has been assassinated somewhere in the Balkans. They anticipate on the basis of this repugnant news item the darkest of European tragedies.

It is sufficient for Mr. Cuffycoat to open the cupboard discreetly and extract a few pinches of Truth therefrom to do justice to that nonsense. The error of Norwood and Clinton is to view the twentieth century through the lens of the age of cave-dwellers or the Hundred Years War. Even assuming that Austria and Serbia conserve a few tiresome atavistic survivals, the great powers are there, on the alert. Peaceful Germany—see Lord Haldane—is there to retain its ally by the sleeve. If France exhibits a residue of nervousness, we have the *Daily News*.

A broad smile cleaves Mr. Cuffycoat's mouth. "Don't worry about it!"

And that evening, at bridge, docile fortune, multiplying honors in his strong hands, ratifies his anticipations and counter-arguments with particular docility.

The World War was not only for Mr. Cuffycoat, as for you and me, the occasion for much private anguish and preoccupations of a general nature. It caused him an appreciable intellectual contrariety.

Naturally, you cannot imagine for an instant, whatever its repercussions might have been, that it had disturbed Mr. Cuffycoat to the point of attempting a vain search to find the key thrown in the Thames from London Bridge, or revising the contents of his cupboard. The Truth has the property that, unlike fish and hollyhocks, it can be preserved indefinitely without there being any need to touch it. A fire-damp explosion costs the lives of two hundred miners; it is a regrettable accident for their families and for the Company, because of matters of pensions and compensation, but it does not devalue the gift that Nature has made to human beings in putting coal at their disposal. The World War is a disagreeable news item. It is as ineffective against the Truth as against universal gravitation. The shock that it has caused so many superficial minds is an opportunity to affirm more energetically in the face of their neurasthenia the principles of the eternal order.

Nevertheless, the best-informed moralists recommend the avoidance not only of sin but of the temptations that clear its path. You might well have enclosed the Truth in a solidly-built cupboard, but beware of woodworm and burglars who might force the lock. Mr. Cuffycoat could not be in doubt that, however imperceptible the European scuffle was from a cosmic viewpoint, and however secondary it appeared from a genuinely philosophical viewpoint, it nevertheless projected into the atmosphere of everyday life all sorts of microbes, complications and annoyances. It filled the newspapers with its news, the streets with its posters, and conversations with its din. It intervened in private life in the form of difficulties with food-supplies and vexatious regulations. It lay in wait for Mr. Cuffycoat at his club. It assailed him in his domestic hearth with neither truce nor repose, from the day when the son of Mrs. Bartle, his housekeeper, was sent to the Flanders front. The first zeppelin raids on London rendered its splatterings even noisier.

The government made every effort to protect the principal public establishments, the banks and the armaments factories, but the Truth is a product far more precious than administrative papers, leases and shells.

Mr. Cuffycoat did not hide from himself for an instant, therefore, that the moment was particularly opportune to undertake a long-planned voyage to Australia. Thus, he would shelter the treasure of which he was the depositary from any unhealthy contact. At the same time, he could complete his research on the customs of primitive peoples, and, associating himself with the patriotic efforts of his countrymen, reassure the populations of Melbourne and Sydney by means of a few lectures with regard to the phases of a worldly accident that was doubtless regrettable, but the importance of which it was necessary not to exaggerate.

Therefore, having instructed Mrs. Bartle to air his apartment for two hours every morning, and informing Norwood and Clinton that he would be absent for a couple of months, he went to Liverpool to embark on the Cunard Company steamer *Merry Mary*, departing for Adelaide.

The first days of the journey were favored by exceedingly fine weather, and the Mediterranean crossing, accomplished in the best possible conditions, permitted Mr. Cuffycoat to ascertain the extent to which the disasters of submarine piracy had been exaggerated by Lord Northcliffe's newspapers. In the Red Sea, he saw several dugongs and a large number of troop-ships. The Indian Ocean did not give rise to any observation on his part worthy of being recorded. At that distance, events in little Europe appeared in their veritable perspective, and he made it his duty to deliver a commentary on it to his neighbors at table, a Scottish lady with and angular profile, who was going to distribute Bibles and trousers to the natives of the islands, and an obese Dutch lady covered in jewels, who was rejoining her husband in various plantations of species,—rice and sugar cane,— whose value had been multiplied tenfold by the war.

It was probably a hundred miles or so from the north-western coast of New Guinea that one of those contingencies intervened that are completely imperceptible from Sirius but the multiplication of which, since August 1914, has significantly increased charter fees and the cost of maritime insurance. In spite of the administrative investigation of which it was the object, the loss of the *Merry Mary* with all hands and cargo has never been fully explained, but it appears incontestable, in view of the fine weather, the absence of any reefs in that region and the on-board prohibition of spirits, that it must be attributed to Boche malfeasance. Either a submarine had succeeded, thanks to criminal complicity, in prolonging its depredations even in those distant seas, until the day when it was definitively sunk, or, more probably, the steamer had encountered a badly-secured mine of a kind forbidden by international treaties but mass-produced in large quantities in the factories of Wilhelmshaven.

The fact is that, forty-five seconds later, everything went to the bottom . . . and like the crew and the rest of the passengers, Mr. Cuffycoat would have concluded his earthly career in that deplorable, but ultimately minor, incident, if he had not chanced, on emerging from the turbulent waters, to perceive an empty chicken cage floating alongside him. He clung on to it with his last reserves of strength and had just recovered his breath when, similarly rising up from the abyss in her turn, the adipose Dutchwoman, stuck a completely bald and repugnant head out of the water, and nearly spoiled everything by trying to climb on to the apparatus as well. It was obviously too frail for two people, and there was no comparison whatsoever between the value of that old lady and the cupboard confided to Mr. Cuffycoat. He therefore delivered a vigorous swing of his fist to the lunar face, which disappeared, and remained bobbing on the waves for hours—long enough for him to lose consciousness completely.

When he recovered his senses he was lying on a beach strewn with fragments of coral, seashells and wreckage, on the edge of which were verdant clumps of mangroves.

A few moments were sufficient for him to take account of the fact that half his body was grievously scratched, that there was blood on his forehead, and that his worldly possessions were limited to his waistcoat, his shirt, torn trousers, two socks and one badly-damaged shoe. In his pocket he had a purse containing twenty shillings, and, thanks to a rubber envelope, his wallet, containing his check book, documents and a few banknotes, was intact. No inn seeming to be close by, Mr. Cuffycoat had to admit that this fiduciary equipment would not procure the same commodities as in the Strand or Oxford Street; and, as he was dying of hunger, disdaining the advice of Dr. Turveymoon, who had advised him formally to avoid crustaceans, he set off in pursuit of crabs, and cracked a good dozen of them between his teeth.

Thus restored, the situation appeared to him in its true light. Without his being exempt from trivial inconveniences, he had an exceptional opportunity to abstract himself from the annoying contingencies that were momentarily obscuring the European firmament, and supplementing the Truth with a host of precious and original observations. No doubt the commerce of the innocent peoples inhabiting this region would reconstitute a link in the invisible but certain chain linking the Golden Age of antiquity, anterior to history but discovered by Rousseau and Aphra Behn,[1] to that of the future, as yet obscured by a few wisps of mist.

Evidently, the vicinity of a grocery and a confectioner's shop would have assisted Mr. Cuffycoat more rapidly to refurbish the cupboard of which he had custody, but heat rendered a simplification of wardrobe tolerable, without any great inconvenience. With some bark and a few lianas, Mr. Cuffycoat improvised a second shoe, and an excellent hat capable of warding off sunstroke. After a few days, with his temporal and spiritual reserves duly reestablished and polished, he set forth.

By the racket of roars that rose up in the nearby forest as soon as darkness fell, he judged it preferable not to plunge into it and to content himself with following the coast, sustaining his strength with oysters, crabs, coconuts—which he found much inferior to their

---

1 Mrs. Aphra Behn's *Oroonoko; or, The Royal Slave* (1688) is the first text discussed in Lichtenberger's study of utopian socialism. The novel's narrator opens the story with a description of the alleged Golden Age in which the simple indigenes of Surinam are allegedly dwelling—or were, before slavers and colonists arrived.

reputation—and seabirds brought down by thrown stones, which reeked frightfully of lamp-oil. Although it would have been more agreeable to see the silhouette of a small hotel or the humblest vending machine, he was pleasantly distracted by the spectacle of several flying squirrels, and noticed with pleasure, unfortunately out of range, a herd of kangaroos.

✳

On the third day, Mr. Cuffycoat went to sleep, as usual, exhausted by fatigue. In the early hours, he dreamed that, at table at the club with Norwood, he served him a few slices of Truth, appropriately seasoned, for which Norwood thanked him by seizing him, as was his habit, by the button of his jacket. Instead of letting him go, however, the sympathetic gentleman's finger dug into his side in an increasingly irritating fashion—to the extent that Mr. Cuffycoat ended up struggling desperately until the moment when he woke up and perceived the flint point of some sort of harpoon on his breast, from whose tip his gaze rose beyond the black fist that held it to envisage the grimacing face of the most abominable Guy Fawkes that the most convinced anti-papist had ever been capable of imagining.

Mr. Cuffycoat hastened to address his best smile to this visitor and a few cordial words of welcome, while a number of his fellows gathered around him, prancing around with horrible capers and sinister howls.

For want of knowing the local language, Mr. Cuffycoat could not follow very exactly the discussion that began, but it was evident that he played an important role therein. A venerable elder who would have delighted maids and babies in the central cage in the Zoo came to examine him with particular attention. When, eventually, he acquired a better understanding of the local folklore, he understood that it had been very much a question of eating him, and that only his thinness and the unusual color of his skin, which gave rise to the fear that he would be difficult to digest, had spared him that form of burial.

They contented themselves with tying his hands behind his back and imprisoning his neck in a fork whose two points were drawn together by a bit beneath his chin. A frightful negro child took hold of the shaft and rained blows upon him every time he attempted to pause in order to get his breath back. It was thus that he was led to the nearby indigenous village, where the women greeted him with a chorus of howls that reminded him unmistakably of a suffragette meeting in Whitechapel.

The life that Mr. Cuffycoat was forced to lead furnished him with a fine opportunity to testify to the degree to which a free thought is capable of raising itself above the perishable rag to which it is attached. If the Truth of which he had taken delivery a quarter of a century earlier had been less thoroughly verified and endorsed, there is no doubt that it would have run a grave risk of stumbling in the course of the adventure.

In fact, the role of the ladies of the country being to serve their husbands as beasts of burden, his own was effectively that of a beast of burden at the disposal of other beasts of burden. With blows from fingernails, teeth and clubs, he was instructed in the arts of pounding grain, skinning game and watching the roasting-spit.

In that capacity, one of the most painful tasks that had been confided to him was that of supervising the cooking of two old men, who formed the main course of a kind of Christmas dinner, the character of which was both religious and exquisitely gastronomic.

Certainly, the fine works of Sir John Lubbock and a few other sociologists had prepared him not to take exception in a puerile fashion to certain customs whose singularity only disconcerts us for want of adequate reflection. Anthropophagy has, as its first principle, a praiseworthy spirit of economy; nothing is as culpable as wasting food. In the second place, it proceeds from a spirit of veneration for our ancestors; what more honorable tomb could be offered to them than the bellies of their posterity? Thirdly, it is beyond doubt that it tends to satisfy an instinct analogous to that of our academic appetite. Having no books to devour in the equatorial region, because of the rudimentary state of printing in that latitude, one assimilates what ought to be therein by preferentially eating the brains of those presumed to be capable of writing them.

Plausible as the philosophical substratum of that doctrine might be, however, it shocked prejudices in Mr. Cuffycoat so deeply anchored that he found a veritable relief in the fact that his humble status prevented him from taking part in the feast. That relief was not such, however, that he did not feel that he had the right to take the first available opportunity to break a contract that, in truth, he had not signed.

By virtue of all the blows, his back was nothing but a single wound, like the spines of donkeys in Arab lands. He was fed in an ignoble manner, with the offal of prey and rotten fish. Glances of which he was the object on the part of two frightful Megaeras gave him glimpses of new perils, of which the example of Joseph shunning the flirtation of Potiphar's wife demonstrated the imperious duty. He did not, therefore, believe himself to be failing in any delicacy one evening when the entire tribe was drunk on palm-wine in freeing himself by filing through his shackles with a trenchant sea-shell, and, having got rid of his fork, making off as rapidly as his legs would carry him.

Having run all night and a part of the morning, without any sign indicating to him that he was being pursued, he conjectured that his hosts had reconciled themselves to his taking "French leave." Spotting a pretty little inlet between the coral reefs where a little stream flowed, he allowed himself to collapse on the edge of a coconut grove and, after having swallowed two or three rancid mouthfuls, went to sleep, exhausted by fatigue.

When Mr. Cuffycoat woke up the sun was already low on the horizon. Suddenly, he had the idea of ending the day by bathing, which would relax his bloody feet and soothe his bruised back. It was, in any case, the time of year when he had the custom of devoting himself to that sport at Brighton, or on one of the beaches of northern France.

He therefore went down to the edge of the sea and was getting ready to take off his rags when an unexpected apparition caused him genuine amazement and caused a supplementary redness to rise to his sunburned cheeks.

In the very edge of the waves, nonchalantly lying on the sand, was a lady whose face, quite pleasant, suggested an age of about forty. Although clad in a rather outmoded manner—it was twenty years since those bell-skirts had been the height of fashion—she was not without some pretention to elegance. Leaning on her elbow, she seemed to be fishing in a box of chocolates with ivory tweezers, although Mr. Cuffycoat determined subsequently that she was merely tickling a holothurian with a shark-bone.

Mr. Cuffycoat had received an excellent education. He was cruelly conscious of the fact that his appearance was insufficiently decent for an introduction. Innocent of any contact with a comb, a brush or soap for more than three months, burned by the sun, covered in wounds and dirt, he must have offered a frightful sight. Besides, the far-from-abundant garments that the shipwreck had left him had suffered the cruelest simplifications since. The truth is that they were reduced to such a minimum that there was hardly anything worth mentioning. How gladly he would have given all the bills in his wallet for a forty-five shilling suit!

In spite of these painful circumstances, he told himself insistently that, in these regions, the first duty of a gentleman was to put himself at the disposal of that lady. So, coughing lightly and bowing decorously, he took two steps forward and expressed the pleasure that he would experience if he might in some way be useful to a lady of standing. At the same time, he excused himself immediately for the incorrectness of his attire. It was very difficult in that latitude to procure the slightest thing . . . but if, by chance, it were possible to give him an address . . .

The lady must have been accustomed to traveling, and possessed of considerable self-control. She did not manifest any disapproval of her interlocutor's wardrobe and even gave evidence of more curiosity than amazement at his appearance. She replied to him immediately in very correct English—she had hardly a trace of a foreign accent—that she was very touched. Certainly there were few resources here. It was a significant stroke of luck to encounter a man of the world. Furthermore, had she not already had the pleasure . . . ?

That was precisely what Mr. Cuffycoat was in the process of asking himself. That accent, that face, even that costume, obsolete but not devoid of pretentions, reawakened distant memories in him . . .

A movement on the lady's part enlightened him. While adjusting her skirt she had just uncovered, instead of feet, a tail: a tail of a very pretty model, with a hint of the mackerel about it, in sparkling colors . . . but, all in all, a tail . . .

Mr. Cuffycoat uttered an exclamation. Abruptly, he remembered a season near Folkestone when he had encountered, in the house of his friends the Buntings, that singular individual unexpectedly sprung from the sea, around whom there was a mystery that was so piquant, and who had turned poor Charteris' head so terribly.

He bowed again. "Miss Waters," he said, "please excuse me if, at first, I didn't recognize you. The unexpectedness of the encounter . . . Cuffycoat, the friend of the worthy Buntings . . . at Sandgate Castle . . .[1]

Miss Waters smiled graciously and blushed slightly. Mr. Cuffycoat was really too kind. Alas, in twenty years, a woman changes a great deal . . .

"Besides which, I must look a perfect fright. One tries to keep up to date. Your fashion magazines, when, by chance, a shipwreck procures some of them for us, arrive so badly damaged by damp, fish, lobsters, and all the rest . . . and our couturiers, you know . . . always demands, strikes, broken promises . . ."

She shook her head dolorously. Mr. Cuffycoat agreed, but with a hint of distraction—for he had experienced an abrupt flash of enlightenment. In sum, it had been a risible error of judgment that had led him to believe that he would find the innocence of primitive humankind in the indigenous populations. All the discoveries of modern science teach us that it is from the sea that universal life emerged. It is there, no doubt, that a special humankind subsists, continuing to practice the virtues from which terrestrial humankind has temporarily departed, but toward which it is returning by means of great strides . . .

In consequence, a delightful plan took sketchy form in his mind while he replied a trifle distractedly to Miss Waters' questions. The Buntings were in very good health. Melville had died some ten years before. Adeline

---

1 Author's note: "See H. G. Wells, *The Sea Lady.*"

Glendower had not married. At present, skirts were very short . . .

In response to the reiterated pleas of his interlocutrice, he even tried to describe the costumes recently glimpsed at a charity auction at a ministry. Unfortunately, he did not know the technical terms. He hazarded: "If you would authorize me to accompany you to your couturier, perhaps I'd be able to explain it by means of a model."

As the siren seemed to be looking at him with some surprise, he judged that he might as well come straight out with it. "Miss Waters," he said, "you'll excuse me, in the circumstances in which I find myself, for speaking frankly . . ."

And, pouring out his heart, he explained all the inconveniences to which the war in the old world had given birth for him, and those that he had just experienced on the part of the Papuans. Painful as the hypothesis was, the precious cupboard—he pointed to himself—in which the essential Truths were contained seemed at risk of deteriorating before long, and—who could tell?—being cleft from top to bottom by some irreparable fissure. By contrast, might not a judicious immersion in the brine render that item of furniture all of its shine and all of its watertightness?

In other terms, he, Cuffycoat, was asking Miss Waters for permission to go home with her, with the hope of savoring in her company the peace of the great depths, of rediscovering the calm, the innocent tranquility that permits the mind . . .

A strident burst of laughter interrupted him.

The peace of the great depths! Tranquility of mind! Alas, Mr. Cuffycoat was surely joking? Yes, undoubtedly, at Sandgate Castle she had put on a show. When one is unfamiliar with the customs of society, one does not bore one's hosts with an account of one's own troubles . . . But submarine existence is a nightmare, something atrocious. Unrelentingly, everywhere, there are battles, massacres, creatures devouring one another . . .

"To go home in a little while, it will be necessary for me to clear a path through the most ignoble gang of octopodes—veritable apaches—you can imagine. And on a daily basis one has to defend oneself against the attacks of sharks. We've been obliged to have our house armored with coral in order to breathe easily there. Even then, the narwhals and the swordfish come to pass their trenchant blades through the interstices. There is not a moment when they are not fighting and killing one another. And hideous and voracious monsters incessantly rise up from the great abysses that are far worse than those ridiculous Boche about which you make so much fuss. It requires all the energy of a woman of the world to conceal the horror of that way of life from you. I cannot depict it any better for you than by confessing that, when I long for a moment of tranquility, it's on land, in the company of humans, that I come in search of it."

On the land . . . in the company of humans . . . tranquility . . .

Mr. Cuffycoat stood there open-mouthed, bewildered. He persisted, timidly: "You truly believe . . . a simple change of air for a few days . . ."

Miss Waters cut him off with a hint of dryness. What would they think at home if she brought a gentleman back to the house? A gentleman dressed like that? Bathers certainly allow themselves all kind of license in their dress, but there is a limit. A young woman—even one no longer young—has to observe certain proprieties. Old Mr. Waters is something of a stickler for etiquette. In any case, one primordial reason dispensed with any other. Miss Waters scanned the gentleman with a sharp gaze.

"Where are your gills?"

"My . . . my gills?"

"Yes, your gills, your breathing apparatus . . . in sum, what you need to respire under water. You don't have any? It's impossible, then—even more impossible than driving an automobile without the chauffeur's permission. I'm sorry . . . but I have to take my leave. If you would be so kind as to lend me a hand . . ."

Striving to put on a brave face, Mr. Cuffycoat did his best to support the beauty. She staggered rather gauchely until she was knee-deep in water. Then she stretched herself out, and drew away with a flick of her tail; then, raising her upper body out of the water one last time, she flashed Mr. Cuffycoat a smile and, with one last wave of the hand, disappeared.

Mr. Cuffycoat remained motionless, disconcerted. Suddenly, he pricked up his ears and shivered. In the peace of the falling dusk, an atrocious howling was beginning to be discernible: the war-cries of the Papuans launched in his pursuit.

In a few bounds he had reached the edge of the great forest . . .

He paused momentarily, for the growls of all the ferocious beasts were already rising from its shadows, where their shiny eyes were gleaming. But for a second time, at closer range, the clamor of the cannibals resounded in his ears. He did not hesitate any longer, and deliberately plunged in among the wild beasts.

It is at this point that we must confess that, greatly to our regret, we lose track of Mr. Cuffycoat.

One would dearly like to know in what manner the inestimable Truth of which he was the depositary was preserved in the jungle, but the rarity of strollers and mailmen in that locality, and the contingencies of submarine warfare, leave us in the most painful uncertainty.

The sole evidence that is perhaps worth the trouble of reporting is that of an Irish sailor picked up two months later in the region by a schooner from Hull. If he is to be believed—and his words must evidently be treated with caution—he had been wandering the island for several weeks after a shipwreck. The most curious thing he saw was a tribe of orangutans whose entire way of life testified to a state of civilization at least equal to that of the aborigines. It had also reduced to slavery several individuals whose facial features bore an unmistakable resemblance to those of Papuans. The strangest one even offered a vague resemblance to less primitive races. In the barking and mewling that constituted his manner of self-expression, it was possible to recognize, at times, the inflections of a European language. Thus, every time that, having been found remiss, he was punished by one of the anthropoids, he was heard to groan at length, and his plaints could be translated exactly by the words "All right; very well," as pronounced by an American who might have had seals in his family.

Is it necessary to establish a connection between that rather suspect deposition and the ultimate destiny of Mr. Cuffycoat? That is a point on which I forbid myself to make a decision. We only suspect that, whatever his fate might have been, he kept inviolate until the end the precious stock of Truth confided to his care, of which rather rich specimens are fortunately conserved in the majority of Academies and scientific bodies of the two worlds.

## NOTE

The editor of this periodical[1] has been kind enough to authorize me to communicate to his readers the story that they have just read, and which was presented to me as coming from the eminent pen of Mr. Wells.

It differs singularly from the most recent stories of the celebrated writer, but it is not without some analogy to his previous publications. It would not, therefore, be impossible that it is a matter of a particularly prophetic

---

1 Author's note: "This fragment first appeared in the *Revue Mondiale*."

"anticipation" of his youth, or even an imperfect draft of a work that he will give us in the next phase of his evolution.

Some exacting mind might perhaps remark that I could easily have settled the question of its origin by addressing myself to Mr. Wells, whose kindness would have informed me. That is a procedure which I flatly refuse.

The work of a genius such as Mr. Wells ceases to belong to the individual and becomes the property of humankind. It would therefore be intolerable that the imperialism of a single individual should decide its tenor. It would not be worth the trouble of having created war and democracy if it were necessary for us to tolerate henceforth such a despotism of the individual. At a time when all the nations of the world are submitting themselves to the universal suffrage of determining their political destinies, it would be pitiful if literary problems of an infinitely narrower range were removed from the judgment of the nation.

I would therefore be glad if the readers of this periodical were to hold a referendum—ladies are naturally admitted—in order to decide whether or not this fantasy belongs to Mr. Wells. If the answer is yes, it will figure, in spite of all his protests, at a modest rank, in his complete works. If the answer is no, it is in vain that it will have been written, from the first line to the last. It will be withdrawn and will remain attached throughout the centuries to the name of the presumed forger whose name is probably: André Lichtenberger.

# THE LAST SIREN

## by Bernard Lazare

THERE was once a castle built on the edge of the
sea on the Mediterranean coast. It stood on sheer
white rocks, and one of its faces gazed perpetually at the
waves, through the profound blue irises of which marine plants caused dark flashes to pass. As the forest died
out at the edge of the strand, the tall and elegant pines
shaded the turrets with their parasols, and their somber
verdure veiled the manor with melancholy, which only
smiled over the waves; thus, the dwelling had a double
aspect, and that duplicity augmented the mystery with
which the terror of the fishermen had surrounded it.
When the wind blew—and in that region its violence
was abominable—the pines, bent over by the tempest,
seemed to want to hug the walls; their needles rattled,
and frightful harmonies were heard beneath the foliage.

On the side of the cliff, a door was pierced in the wall
of the castle, from which a stairway descended toward
the waves, as if to await the gilded galley of a princess
who would arrive one day. The water was tumultuous
against the granite; one divined profound fissures hol-

lowed out under the reefs, vast grottoes in which gods were perhaps asleep.

The manor had been deserted for many years. The ivy had caused the battens of the doors to yield beneath its embrace; it had dislocated the stones and broken the steps of the seigneurial perron. Along the pathways in the gardens and the orchards, the carpet of fallen leaves had thickened in the solitude, and it extended its smooth bronze sheet, which no human foot had ever soiled. Giant rose-bushes, iron virgins, had raised their hedges around orange and lemon trees, and jasmine bushes leaned on the trunks of almond trees.

The castle was protected by legend and dread. It had once been inhabited by a noble and ancient family, and the local mariners and peasants related a troubling story about the hereditary lords. According to them, no one had ever seen the eldest sons of the Barons de Torsis, as they were called, succeed their fathers, thus inheriting the titles and privileges of the house. The heirs of the Torsis were always younger sons, and the eldest always perished in a similar fashion. When they reached twenty years of age, they were found, one morning in May, lying on the steps of the stairway leading down to the sea. They bore no wound; no spasm had twisted their limbs or convulsed their face; they seemed to be asleep in death, the eyes partly open, shining and ecstatic, the arms curved inwards as if in a grip, but on the mouth was a bloodstain, like the bite of a kiss.

One day, the Torsis had abandoned their manor, fleeing before destiny. They had closed the doors of that tomb, and since then, none of them had returned, even to honor the memory of the dead Torsis who reposed beneath the marble slabs, under the eternal vigil of the baying waves, which beat the walls of the crypt with their silver helmets. Since then they had lived at the court; some had distinguished themselves in embassies, one as a minister, others had become illustrious in the camps; there was even a renowned general among them.

After their departure from the castle, fate had been favorable to them, and the eldest sons of the Torsis had been able to perpetuate their race. Nevertheless, one of them still perished mysteriously. He was a mariner, and one evening when he was returning from the lands of the Orient his ship stopped before the family dwelling, which appeared to him in the distance, bloody in the sunset. His companions related afterwards that at the sight of the disquieting turrets, a shadow of melancholy had paled the forehead of that Torsis. He had leaned on the rail and contemplated for a long time the pines inflamed by the sunlight; then, when night fell, he sat down in the poop and asked to be left alone. He was obeyed, and when dawn came it was seen that he was still sitting on his bench; his crimsoned lips let no breath pass; he was dead. Thus, once again, the younger son of the family inherited the title, but he was the last to cause the lineage to deviate.

Centuries of abandonment had passed over the castle when it reawakened to life. One spring day, the fishermen saw the house invaded; crews of workmen had come from the city to trouble the silence of the marvelous gardens and the peace of the vast halls. The rose-bushes, the ivy and the jasmine were mutilated by adroit gardeners; the steps of the disrupted perron were consolidated; the pines that held the walls prisoner with the network of their branches were driven back, and fresh air traversed the neglected chambers, the corroded drapes of which fell apart in the saline air.

When the castle was furnished, and the park and orchard had resumed their beautiful order, the master arrived. He arrived at dusk, and his horses could barely fray a passage through the surprised crowd that gathered to see the frail and sad young man who had returned to the seat of his ancestors. He was the last of the Barons de Torsis; at twenty years of age he remained alone, having never had a sister or a brother, and his father and mother having died, undermined by the malaise that attacks old lineages to excess.

When René de Torsis crossed the threshold, those who had accompanied him thus far sensed a vague anguish grip them, for, as the sun disappeared over the horizon, a trail of blood ran over the waves and came to attain the last step of the legendary stairway that faced the sea. Only René did not tremble, and a sort of joy illuminated his face as he entered the vestibule ornamented with mosaics.

He had a light collation served; after having eaten he sent away his domestics and penetrated the bedroom that he had chosen, one of those whose windows overlooked the water. He cast a distracted glance over the tapestries and the furniture, nodded his head, as if the décor pleased him, and then came to lean on the balustrade, looked down at the rocks, and lost himself in a dream.

He had lived alone until his twentieth year, pursuing sad dreams during his youth and adolescence. He had been born deprived of everything, and had been ignorant of joys as of dolors, his existence having been one long torment. He had never experienced anything but a heavy lassitude; he bore on his feeble shoulders the burden of ages past, and at the moment when he knew a desire it was the desire for death, mingled with a desire for amour. Women were, however, indifferent to him; his eyes had not opened to their beauty, and it was vague phantoms that trouble his sleep. An imprecise, mysterious sentiment invaded him, however; he felt summoned. He knew the history of his family; old servants had related it to him and he had often shivered in his childhood at the repeated tale.

As he had grown older, a preoccupation with those somber adventures had developed, but gradually, he had forgotten the details; only one had subsisted, the obsession of which increased with the years and oppressed him entirely. Soon, he only thought of one thing: the mouths of the corpses, each mouth bloodied by a kiss, terrible but so sweet that it killed. One day, he could no longer resist the attraction of death; he decided to return to the castle that gave forgetfulness, and he departed, going toward his bride.

He thought about all that while darkness fell. In the distance, the moon paled the waves; he watched the star rise, and while it shed its blond light, he listened to the floating harmonies. Little by little, they became more precise, accumulating, and he heard a voice.

What was it saying? Doubtless he understood the strange words, for he got up abruptly, traversed the dormant corridors, arrived at the low door that opened on to the cliff, opened it without hesitation and remained motionless on the threshold.

The voice reached him more distinctively and more seductively. It was the summons. Radiant with jubilation and tenderness, he set foot on the top step of the stairway leading down to the sea and, as he was about to descend, he saw her. She emerged from the white wave, lifting her golden hair with her alabaster arms, spilling marine peals over her breast. She continued singing without looking at him.

Suddenly, she raised her eyes toward him: green eyes, abyssal eyes.

He held out his arms and said: "Here I am."

"Here I am," she replied. "I was expecting you."

As if he were obeying an order, René lay down on the steps, and she went on: "You had to come and I had to see you. Without you, life was weighing upon me. Alas, it has been too long, my life, since the day when, on the Erythrean Sea, the frightful voice cried the death of Pan. I have survived my sisters, and here, in the Neptunian grottoes, people have forgotten me. My voice always made itself heard in the meantime, but men were not listening, they did not understand my songs, and my agonizing beauty. Why did those of your race understand my words? Doubtless it was a favor of destiny. I have had the most handsome of your family for lovers, until the dolorous moment when their senses too were veiled and when they fled, forsaking me.

"I have lived in spite of everything, for I hoped for their return. One of them came to seek me one evening, with his flag-decked gallery, and then, abandoned again, I let the hours go by in waiting. You have come, finally, the last of your line, and after you, no one will come. You are the most fortunate of all the Torsis. Your brothers died of my kiss, but tonight, I shall die of yours, while you faint under the caress of the last of the Sirens."

In her turn, she extended her arms toward him; inclining like a flower, he came to fall upon the beloved breast; their lips met, and as the moon came to kiss the granite, the last Torsis and the last Siren expired, enlaced.

# AN AMOROUS ADVENTURE
# AT SEA

## by Henri de Régniér

M Y turbulent childhood soon gave way to a difficult youth, but the former was forgiven when
the latter brought me to embark, at the age of seventeen,
on the *Sans-Pareil*, which bore the flag of your uncle
the Admiral. The squadron was about to sail when my
father took me to the harbor. From the inn, I followed
him through the streets, where he sometimes turned
around to make sure that I had not given him the slip,
for he feared some escapade that might thwart his opportunity to get rid of me.

The quays were overflowing. Stevedores, bending
their backs beneath the weight of boxes, were elbowing
their way through the crowd. Sweat was pouring from
sunburnt foreheads and saliva dripping from the corners
of mouths. The corpulence of barrels protruded over the
flagstones where the obesity of sacks collapsed. People
stepped over chains only to get tangled in ropes. The
long gangplanks connecting the ships to the shore were
sagging in the middle under the feet of porters. Vessels
filled the dock.

Here and there, amid the network of yard-arms overlapped, a hoisted sail inflated, and the masts were oscillating imperceptibly against the blue of the sky. There was an assembly of ships of all kinds, painted red, green and black, shining with varnish or dull with wear. Bulging hulls brushed against sleek flanks, the former swelling like goatskins, the latter tapering like rockets. Figurines were profiles at the prows, grimacing masks fashioning emblems. Carved into the wood, one could see the face of a goddess, the visage of a saint or the muzzle of an animal. Mouths were smiling in the snouts, the whole being barbarous, naïve or ridiculous. Holds exhaled the odor of food-supplies and the perfume of spices; the cargoes mingled the sharpness of pickling-brine with the perfume of tar.

A small boat picked up my father, me and my luggage, to take us to the squadron anchored outside the harbor. We wove our way through the inextricable clutter of the docks; the rhythmically-plied oars sometimes brought up a piece of seaweed or peel. The stagnant salt-water was adulterated with all kinds of filth, marbled by oily patches, sticky with viscosities. Gradually, progress became easier, the obstacles more widely spaced; we went around a few large vessels with pot-bellies. Squatting heavily, streams of dirty water dribbled from the muzzles of their prows; the smoke of galleys rose in spirals around the masts; a cabin-boy perched in the rigging threw a rotten apple at us as we passed by. I picked it up and saw in the purulent flesh the marks of the teeth with which the joker was laughing at us, sitting astride a yard-arm.

The boat began to sway gently, and once the pier had been doubled we perceived the squadron; it was gathered there, high on the blue sea. Four ships, and one larger one, slightly apart. We steered for the *Sans-Pareil*. A flag bearing a coat of arms was flapping at the top of the mainmast. The muzzles of the cannon were gleaming in the gun-ports. The masts cast slender shadows on the calm water. A bell rang.

The rowers made haste, bent over their oars. A little foam splashed my hands. We were spotted, and climbed aboard by means of a rope-ladder. We were just in time. The anchors were being raised by rotating capstans; the ships were about to get under way. I was left alone; my father hurried off to talk to the admiral. The departure cut short our goodbyes. Whistle-blasts overlapped; commands were shouted through a loud-hailer. The extended sails inflated. My father got back into the launch. We waved to one another; we never saw one another again.

A brutal altercation, my exit, slamming the door, a day of anger wandering through the countryside, the asperity of the landscapes neighboring the château, the high winds of that scorching summer, the promptitude of an arrogant character, the impetuosity of an intractable pride, all came back to me, along with the paternal insult whose ineptitude I grasped: the lost head, enraged hands and furious fanaticism that had broken, methodically and angrily all the windows on the ground floor of the château with hurled stones, so that a shard of glass struck the head of the cellar-master and broke the cup that my father was holding, at the table from which the women got up in fear and fled.

The gardeners found me the next day, lying in the bushes, nursing the intoxication of my folly. Those worthy men, who had grown old in our service, were not unduly surprised by the outburst. They doubtless saw it as a continuation of my precocious misdeeds: opened bird-cages, trampled flower-beds, broken fences and, once, the most beautiful roses in the garden savagely cut and scattered on the path.

I was seven years old then. I had been removed from the care of the women and tutors succeeded one another, intermittently, from one month to the next. I saw their strange faces again. There were fat ones and thin ones, bulging bellies and rigid spines, in ecclesiastical garb or with a learned deportment, the worn faces of aged deacons and the hollow faces of young laymen, some reeking of the sacristy and others of the library. Of them all, the memory remains of looking forward to my liberty, a little Latin, not much Greek, no mathematics, a few shreds of history, and of one of them, whom I rather liked and who ended up as a poet somewhere, precise notions of mythology, with a knowledge of the gods, their attributes and their amours.

Mine soon commenced. Mansards and barns sheltered the enterprises. Chambermaids' straw mattresses and pastoral bundles of hay lent themselves to my first frolics. I remember summoning bells interrupting the games and barking dogs disconcerting the positions. I put my arms round ancillary waists and fondled rustic breasts. The affectations of ladies' maids varied the naivety of shepherdesses. To the jargon of the former and the patois of the latter I soon preferred the daughters of the nearby town.

It was one of them, and the scandal of an excessively loud love-making session, that occasioned, after an ill-tempered reprimand, the altercation whose consequences I could mull over at leisure aboard the *Sans-Pareil*, and in the fresh wind that raised her up, along with the swell, on the high seas.

Sculpted on her prow, the *Sans-Pareil* bore a mariner's face, winged and scaly, painted in gold, and on her poop, each holding aloft a lantern with swirling flame, were four genies blowing the breath of their gilded mouths into twisted seashells.

Birds the color of oriental waters and the white grebes of icy seas whirled around our errant beacon lights. The mariner's head was mirrored in calm waves or splashed by tumultuous waves. The tropical sun cracked its horny gilt and the moon of polar nights silvery its icy smile. Its staring eyes saw the curves of gulfs and the angles of capes; its ears heard the nonchalant harmony of waves lapping sandy beaches and the crash of surf on rocky promontories.

Many strange peoples came aboard. We received bearded men in garments of oily leather. Without saying a word, they brought us reindeer horns, seals' teeth and bearskins. Ceremonious yellow dwarfs presented us with silkworm cocoons, bright ivory, lacquer-work, and insects and grotesques carved in jade like frogspawn. Negroes offered us feathers lightly powdered with gold, and, on one isolated island, we saw green-tinted women coming toward us dancing and juggling red sponges.

For four years I traveled the seas in that fashion. The anchor bit into the coral of madrepores and the granite of reefs. The wind that inflated our sails had the odor of sunlight or snow. We took on fresh water on every shore. The salt water of marshes and the clear water of stony brooks left their mud or sand in the bottom of goatskins in their turn.

I visited many ports: those which swarm under the sun, those which get bogged down under the rain and those which go to sleep under the snow, which contain great ships, protect painted boats or only shelter a few bark canoes. Cities appeared to us at dawn and dusk, magnificent or lamentable, heaping up the rows of their palaces or crowding the huddled mass of their shacks, those from which one heard the sound of orchestras by night and those in which one heard the voices of fisherman hauling in their nets at dusk.

We saluted doges in marble dwellings and obis in mud huts. In sordid dives we slaked ourselves with black slaves; in luxurious bedrooms we courted bejeweled women. Smoky torches and bright candelabras shone over our sleep.

Thus I came to know all the seas. We escorted princes and joined merchant convoys. Sometimes our gun-ports roared. Sulfurous smoke floated, unleashing golden lightning. I felt the quivering of broadsides and the shock of cannonballs smashing into the hull, torn sails hanging down from broken masts. I saw ships sunk, by pirates' fire-ships as well as corsairs' grapnels.

The sea is even more terrible than those who bloody it. I've seen all its faces—its infantile morning face, its gold-streaming midday face, its Medusan evening mask and its shapeless nocturnal aspects, the insidiousness of calms succeeded by the vehemence of tempests. A god inhabits the changing water; he sometimes rises up, taking hold of the mane of the waves and the tresses of the algae, in the rattle of the wind and the rumor of the swell; he fashions himself out of foam and mist; his mysterious hands clench like claws; and, standing up, with his waterspout torso, his mantle of fog, his face of cloud and his lightning-flashing eyes, he works his magic on the waves and the squalls and, innumerable, collapses in the monstrous baying of the waves, the howling of muzzles and the laceration of talons, succumbing in the racket of his fall and reborn in the dribble of his own fury.

The sea was uniformly calm and mild when we arrived in the vicinity of the island of Lérente. We had come from far away, a long crossing over misty waters. The ice-floes were melting as we entered that warmer region; the sky gradually cleared and the sun reappeared. The crimson flag was rippling in the breeze; the figure on the prow was reflected in a mirror continually broken before it by the rapidity of the course that dispersed its crystal. One day, at sunset, the lookout cried: "Land!" The coast appeared momentarily, in green and roseate glory, and as dusk fell a damp fog enveloped the vessel and covered the sea around us. We were sailing slowly over violet water in the gentle moistness of those airborne tissues, translucent and crumpled.

The pilot steered with circumspection. The landing was dangerous, the point notorious for shipwrecks. A vague superstition surrounded the famous and charming island, divine and once siren-haunted.

Suddenly, the *Sans-Pareil*, her sails hauled in, completed her course and stopped; the anchor bit; the fine spidery mist clung to the masts, hanging down in curtains.

The island was almost invisible. Gradually, an exquisite odor of trees and flowers spread.

The order that everyone had to remain aboard cut short our curiosity. No one was to go ashore that night. The island's noises reached from a distance, as if filtered by the mist.

My companions went to bed, one after another. Everything went quiet. I leaned on the side, listening to the imperceptible oscillation of the masts and the footsteps of a sentinel, and kept my ear cocked toward the shadows. Later, it seemed to me that I could hear music. It sang delightfully in the distance, in an intermittent fashion, as if insinuating itself through the pores of the fog, which muffled the spongy darkness. In the end, I distinguished a concert of flutes.

My resolution was quickly made. The pilot told me that the ship was anchored in the center of a sandy bay, five hundred fathoms from the coast. I went down to my cabin, hung a small compass around my neck and ran to the prow of the vessel, above the figurehead. Undressing rapidly, I took my bearings one last time, and let myself slide silently down an uncoiled rope into the sea.

*

The water was warm and calm, and I swam without making any noise. Soon, the ship disappeared from view. The waves murmured in my ears; sometimes, I floated on my back in order to verify my direction. Soon I heard the rumor of the breakers on the beach. The fog cleared and became a transparent vapor. I found my footing. Floating seaweed brushed my bare legs. The odor of riverside flowers mingled with the aroma of marine plants.

A little wood formed a black mass. It came down to the sea, where the whiteness of a marble terrace was visible. A stairway went down to the water. The steps were draining slowly. A statue of a woman stood up to either side; as the ebb-tide uncovered their waists it made two sirens of them. The polished scales of their tails moistened my hands. I approached each of them in turn and, hoisting myself up, kissed each one on the lips. Their mouths were cool and salty.

I climbed the steps. At the top, I stopped. A star was shining above the trees; wide pathways opened in their thickness. I followed the middle one; it ended at a round-point bordered by arcades of bushes, under which the jets of fountains fell back.

In the center, in a large nacreous shell, a woman was asleep. The water that was running down a rocky wall behind her left pearly drops on her cheeks and breasts. She was lying down, one arm beneath her head, stretched out in the shell, appropriate to her marine slumber. There was a nocturnal half-light, in which her long glaucous dress sparkled. She was smiling in her sleep.

Her smile awoke beneath my kiss. The undulant shell was soft to our united bodies. I took her; a sigh inflated her throat, her hair came loose and silently, in the translucent and perfumed shadows, to the murmur of the fountains, spontaneously and for a long time, she possessed, perhaps the naked image of her dream, and I the mysterious goddess of the embalmed isle.

"Who are you?" she asked me, in a whisper, as she put up her hair again, the damp ends of which had stuck to her excited breasts. "Who are you, who comes mysteriously into private gardens in this fashion, to awaken nonchalant sleepers? Where have you come from? Your lips have the salty taste of the sea and your body a divine nudity. Why did you choose the darkness to appear?

"The marine gods have long been masters of this isle, so survey your domain. I have constructed this retreat to the glory of Love and the Sea. From my terrace, one can see everything. The high tides mingle their fleecy foam with the dove-down of my trees. The wind seems to unfurl in the harmonious treetops. One might think that the raucous and iridescent waves were cooing like turtle-doves.

"I have ornamented my gardens with sea-shells and fountains and erected on the steps of my threshold statues of the Sirens that once dwelt here. Was it them who sent you to me, their sister? I am terrestrial, alas, but the swell of my breasts moves to the rhythm of the waves, the waves of my hair imitate the undulation of algae, my fingernails resemble pink seashells. I am smooth and saline, and this glaucous dress is so limpid that I appear in it as if it were water running continuously over my body."

She smiled as she spoke thus, and then fell silent, and put a finger to her lips.

At the same instant the flutes sang in the illuminated boscage; lanterns lit up in the trees; footfalls and laughter were heard.

We both rose to our feet; something drew me to her ankle and I picked up a long strand of seaweed, which I coiled around my waist. The end of the pathway brightened. Capering torch-bearers preceded a procession of richly-costumed men and women. Silken hoods inflated to the beating of fans. The masquerade spread out into the gardens. The torches were reflected by the fountains. The jets of water scintillated like vaporized gems. The entire wood vibrated with music.

The beautiful nymph had put a hand on my shoulder and, extending the other toward the bizarre crowd surrounding us, she cried out in a clear voice:

"Honor the god, our guest; he came from the stairway to the Sea, to the pious courtesan Sirena de Lérente, who was asleep. He kissed the Sirens of the marine portal on the lips, and his mouth whispered his name to me. He is our guest."

And both of us, interlaced, preceding the musicians and the assembly that was acclaiming us, went along the pathway where the fountains and the flutes were singing to the palace, as dazzling as a magical submarine grotto, where the foam of silverware unfurled on sumptuous tables, and crystal chandeliers hung like stalactites from the ceiling.

And, naked, grave and joyful, I raised to my lips, after she had steeped her own there, a beautiful golden cup worthy of Amour, which had the form of a breast.

# THE PENSIVE LADY

## by Remy de Gourmont

SHE resembled closely enough one of those dark-haired virgin saints, arranged in an attitude of distracted melancholy. Her eyes, of a velvet blackness and a moist softness, always gave the impression of considering with astonishment a rare spectacle invisible for all other eyes; but she only ever gazed afterwards, when there was nothing more at which to gaze, at the beings and things that passed before her. Often, one could even speak to her, or touch her, without her perceiving it; she was one of those women who never know where they are, and never know where they are going.

She had married as if in a dream, less occupied with her husband than with the chimera whose flight she thought she was following, amid the possible landscapes and the skies open to her imagination. Throughout her life she wondered how she had become a woman, doubtless initiated while a wind of inconceivable perfumes enveloped her with unconscious delights.

As she also spoke very rarely, her soul always remained obscure, even for the benevolent wills most determined to force the door of the tabernacle, and it was said of

Aline that she lived like a flower, or the Daphne of the *Metamorphoses*, mute and verdant.

A creature made to be loved, she was loved, like an icon, with a religious respect. People brought her the small presents that please simulacra, and her chapel, like a renowned sanctuary, was ornamented with garlands and ex-votos left by cured or consoled pilgrims. She was truly pacifying; her calm and her serenity soothed anxious hearts, and stained souls recovered their purity in being steeped in the dew of her soft black eyes.

By means of such gifts, she recognized love and compensated it; indiscreet desires stopped a few paces away from her, like superstitious brigands, and fell to their knees; the less fearful kissed the hem of her dress; not one of them had yet dared to lift it.

Every year, leaving her husband, a unique priest, to his affairs, the idol abandoned the sanctuary and went, a pilgrim in her turn, toward the dunes and the waves. Relatives welcomed her, proud of her imagistic beauty, and for months she ornamented the region, a Madonna on vacation.

She departed with her children, with the air of a Laure thinking about her Petrarch, the pensive Lady, and the train carried her away, unaware of landscapes, noises and the petty annoyances of travel. She arrived: the sea! The sea, fatherland of dreams! Aline, a living dream, found brethren among the melancholy pines rustling eternally in the sea breeze.

The dunes were her garden; all day long, she walked in the lukewarm sands, or, fatigued, lay down in the thin grass in the sheltered hollows. Violent or pacific,

near or distant, murmurous or roaring, the sea sometimes frightened the pensive Lady, by obliging her to
pay attention to it; the sea wanted her to gaze at it, the
sea wanted her to listen to it, the sea forced Aline to
emerge from her dream, the sea was jealous, the sea
wanted to be loved; Aline was frightened and fled into
the dunes; crouched in the sand, like an ant-lion, but
innocent, she remained motionless for hours, smiling—
smiling angelically—attracting to her by means of her
breath the invisible reveries, tiny creatures, of which the
air is full.

Aline was happy, for she was alone. No matter how
scantly she felt them, contacts made her suffer, at least
afterwards, by reaction; the idea that someone had just
touched her, or even spoken to her, caused her, if not a
pain, at least an embarrassment. In the street, the gazes
of "impure passers-by" had sometimes given her, on days
of nervousness, the impression of a net of dirty cords
that she had to break in order to pass through; here,
enveloped by solitude, she was not soiled or touched
by the desires of any individual, and in the absolute
absence of sensations, folded entirely upon herself, sure
that no contrary fluid would come to trouble the pure
current of her eternal dream, Aline rose up almost as
high as ecstasy.

A woman made to be loved—but above all to be
divined, closed under the stone veils of the cloister;
doubtless destined for the most intoxicating amours!
Not to act, not to speak; sometimes to sing; that is the
ideal of more than one person; it was Aline's ideal; and
her veritable vocation.

In her phases of solitary ecstasy, Aline sometimes sang; it was a sort of joyful lament emerging from unconscious lips, a rhythmic chant, like that of the sirens, over the respiration of the sea.

She sang, and a fisherman coming back, chased by the rising tide, heard the song of the siren, the joyful lament of the pensive Lady; astonished, he pricked up his ears, accustomed to perceive the slightest nuances of the song of the wind in the pines; he had never heard such a song—he, who knew all the songs of the sea, for whom the foolish sirens had inflated their lungs and broken their conches; he got his bearings, he searched, and in a hollow in the dunes, he perceived Aline.

She was lying on her back, scarcely clad; her light white dress scarcely made a mist over her limbs, and her upper body was affirmed, held by her folded arms. Aline was charming, and a true siren thus posed on the sand, like a delectable wreck borne there by a caprice of the wind; her black hair spread out like wrack, truly similar to the algal tresses of sirens. The fisherman, still damp with sea-water, approached the apparition and caressed it with his heavy hand.

Aline was still singing, departed in a dream, ecstatic, her eyes closed; the fisherman, with his heavy hand, took possession of the wreck. Aline was still singing; the fisherman kissed the siren on the shoulder respectfully, as he had seen the priest kiss the altar before the sacrifice, because he was emotional and religious before such a beauty. Aline was still singing; the fisherman completed his work—and he saw clearly that she was not a siren, for no siren allowed herself to be approached so closely, and none ever risked conceiving of a man.

Aline stopped singing; the pensive Lady awoke, shivering, got up, her mouth bitter from the kiss that had stopped on her lips the flight of her dream song.

The fisherman fled, frightened; she seized him by the hand; he obeyed and listened.

"Why have you stolen me? I belonged to one alone, and his chain was gentle to me because I did not feel its weight. To belong to one alone is still to be free, for that one can love her—which is to say, to assimilate her to himself, to dissolve her in himself . . . but you, stranger, you have weighed upon my heart with all your weight, you have bruised me, you have been my master; from this moment on I am your mistress. Come, we shall wash ourselves together of the crime you have made me commit. Do you hear the voice of the sea—the sea that I love and of which I am afraid? She is calling to us and advancing to meet us; come! Why have you stolen me? I am one whom one does not steal twice; I am the treasure that is animated, that agitates, that twists and coils like an invincible serpent around the neck of the thief; come!"

And the pensive Lady, awakened from her dream, rose up, terrible, inhuman, implacable, and, taking the fisherman by the hand, she went with him toward the sea, dragging him like a little child.

The pensive Lady went into the sea.

# THE SORROW OF THE SIRENS

## by Catullle Mendès

ONE day, when I was going along the sea shore, I heard the sirens lamenting in the blue solitude, in the melancholy moonlight.

"Alas! Alas!" they said. "The times are no more when the handsome young men of the land, lulled by our appeals, bewildered by our whiteness, glimpsed beneath the diaphanous mystery of the water, followed us into the depths and died of our kisses on floating beds of seaweed. It is in vain that, risking ourselves near the shores, we sing in the dusk, enlacing our raised arms; no one listens or stops, and our disdained sighs mingle until dawn with the vague plaint of the waves."

As I listened attentively, I distinguished among the voices one voice more sorrowful, which said:

"Every evening, out there, between the two rocks, a window is illuminated, and I see, through the shadow and the curtains, a form with his head inclined over a book. I recover hope, I glide through the waves, I approach the light, hoisting myself over the sand, tearing my pale flanks and my breasts on the shingle.

"'Hear me, solitary worker, who is consuming the nocturnal hour of kisses in sterile efforts! There is no human reality that is worth as much as the chimera of my amour! Quit deceptive books! Scorn vain science! It is in my glaucous eyes that you will read the sweetest of secrets; my mouth will reveal to you the mystery of joy. Oh, come! I will teach you the languor in which bitter thought becomes somnolent; the cradle of my arms is one of waves of delectable forgetfulness.'

"But the one I summon remains motionless, with his elbows on his table; disdainful, he pays no more heed to my supplicant tenderness than the moans of the squall or the beating of the wings of a dazzled seagull against his window."

The voice fell silent. Another rose up, even sadder, saying:

"One night in summer, I saw in the bow of a ship a man leaning over the side, watching the tremor of the sky in the sea. As he was very young, with a softness in his gaze, I thought that his heart would not be cruel, and, floating on my back, with my arms behind my neck, displaying the enchantments of my luminous torso, I spoke to him amid the smooth sounds of the foam and the water.

"'Are you contemplating me, you who are dreaming? Am I not more beautiful than your dreams? Is there a star in the azure that you prefer to the double roseate star illuminated in the whiteness of my breasts, and what sky reflected in the sea is worth the infinite space of my green eyes? In the distant lands to which your ship is carrying you, there is no fruit more flavorsome than my kissed lips; no siesta is as sweet, in the sunlit forests, amid the warm perfumes and chirping nests, than slumbering beneath my hair, to the sound of my giggles and whispers. Oh, come, you who are exiling yourself, into an exile more charming than any fatherland, in the unknown world of ineffable delights!'

"But the one I was summoning did not interrupt his reverie; he continued leaning over the bow of the ship, with the immensity before him and bales of merchandise behind him, stacked on the deck. And then I realized that he was not watching the sky trembling in the sea, but counting, by the light of the stars, gold coins clinking in an open bag."

Another voice made itself heard in the desolate silence of the moonlight.

"Full of the sound of a host and resounding with the cash of weapons, a ship greater than any other ship was traversing the tumultuous sea; the light of dawn, amid the clinking of bronze, was scattered over the helmets and the sabers in a thousand flashes of steel; and we, like a flock of seagulls, beating the air with our arms, to which the foam lent wings, enveloped the moving ship with our enlaced games and our laughter, which rang joyously in the din of the waves.

"Oh, the madmen! Where were they going? Toward a battle? Toward hideous death? 'What! For the vain chimeras that men call honor, glory and the fatherland, so many young hearts will cease to beat, and so many mouths will know no other kiss than that of pale death? Is there no couch more pleasant than fields of carnage, soaked in mud and blood?

"'But you don't believe us young men! Far from wars, fatigues, and sterile triumphs, you could come with us, so blonde and so tender; you could prefer to rude hand-to-hand combats the caresses of our unarmed nudities. Oh, come! We are beauty, amour and joy. O killers, we are life. Is not the blood of our mouths more beautiful than the blood of wounds? If you require combats, accept those in which victory is certain—certain and so delectable. Triumph over us, warriors! There is no booty worth as much as our bare breasts and our open arms, and after our fortunate defeats, it is in kisses that we, as prisoners, will pay our ransom!'

"But the armed men considered us without tenderness, rejecting us with a scornful gesture. As I clung on to the side of the ship, I felt the cold bite of a steel blade in my arm raised for an embrace, and I fell back into the waves, whose foam was red."

Having heard these things, I said to the sad sirens:

"Don't hope for me to feel compassion for you, dangerous temptresses. Men, having become serious, assiduously occupied with their duties or their business affairs, turn away from you with reason; they are not unaware that you have what is required to trouble the most resolute souls, to disrupt the most useful plans; neither the scholar, nor the merchant, nor the soldier, no one, if he listened to you, would follow his path. We also know, and know above all, how brief the intoxication is that you promise us. O cruel liars, death is the aftermath of your kisses."

The sirens replied:

"It is true that we are redoubtable. It is our dearest game to wear away with our caresses the virile pride of energies. It is true that we are perfidious. Our lovers die in our first embrace. But what mad and despicable race are you, then, new men, who prefer the imbecile vanity of human tasks, and judge that a kiss is not worth dying for?"

# THE SIRENS NO LONGER SING

## by Renée Vivien
## or Hélène de Zylen de Nyevelt

ERMENTRUDE'S youth was studious and taciturn. She only took pleasure in the faded realms of olden days and books. She lived therein a radiantly distant life, wandering over unknown meadows among unreal forms. When winter traced pale arabesques on the windows, she did not see the snow flowering the world, for she was laughing at a summer of dreams ablaze with roses, where lilies consumed their perfumes. When spring sparkled in accordance with the indecisive laughter of the sun, she carried within her the melancholies of an artificial autumn.

The joys and dolors accorded to her by the magic of books enfevered her entire existence, which was externally serene. She was submissive mentally to beautiful tumults of amour and despair. She savored mentally the bittersweetness of renunciation and the cruelty of triumph. She bathed in the indecisive dawn of uncertainties and expectations. She traversed multiple existences and put on a thousand dissimilar souls. Alive, she had lain down in the shadow of death. Like Alcestis, she had returned, weary and mute, from long darkness.

Above all, Ermentrude sought the illusion of verses, more musical than streams, more imperious than the tides, more prismatic than fountains. The poems that charmed her most subtly were those whose imprecise verbiage prolonged an echo of the beyond; for she loved vaguely-sensed but uncomprehended anguishes, and even more indeterminate ecstasies.

Her nostalgic spirit drew her toward vanished Hellas. She was the pious Belated of temples and legends.

Hera appeared to her, white under the glorious curve of the rainbow. At the feet of the goddess, a peacock opened the splendor of its ocellated adornment. Subjugated lightning bolts, tormented the creases of the snowy robe in which the divine body was flamboyant, Hera, who unleashes storms by shaking her black hair, smiled at the child. And Pallas favored her with the gaze of her eyes, as gray and green as the immortal olive trees. For her, Hermes made a lyre from a turtle shell again, and Phoebus Apollo revealed himself to her in golden laughter. But the best realization of her unconscious dream within the sunshine of Myths was the tempting apparition of the Sirens.

"*You will find in your route the Sirens; they enchant all men who come close to them. Those who have the imprudence to approach them and listen to their songs cannot avoid the charm of them, and their wives and children never go to greet them and rejoice in their return. The Sirens retain them in a vast meadow by means of the sweetness of their songs.*"

With a tender precision, Ermentrude evoked those daughters of the foam, those white sisters of the waves, gemmed with reflections and must, and girdled with roseate algae.

One day, Ermentrude's studious life was brightened by a little living sunlight. The young girl was taken to the blue and black Mediterranean, which was the cradle of the Sirens. She loved that sea, which carried so many imperishable memories in its feeble tides.

Pines with curious and tenuous needles raised their violet trunks on the mountainsides. Through their ingeniously-wrought branches, the religious sunset allowed the incandescence of stained glass to pour. They bore strange jagged fruits and a simple perfume of resin. Ermentrude admired the rude slenderness and the heroic grace of those northern trees, which neighbored palm trees and aloes.

The villa where Ermentrude had taken refuge overlooked the sea. Sometimes, the angry waves launched the mist of their crests toward the young girl's windows. Dominating her calmest slumbers, she heard the rumor of the sea. The hissing and rolling of the shingle, drawn one moment and thrown back the next, seemed to her to resemble a great breath abruptly resumed. And because she cherished the sea and legends, she remained leaning on the terrace for a long time, evoking the vanished Sirens.

"Stop your ship in order to hear our voice. No one has passed before this island in a black vessel without first having listened to our melodious voices."

Not far from the coast, a smooth brown rock extended. The waves broke upon it with a white frisson of surf. The rock was shiny and polished, like onyx or agate. In truth, it resembled a marine couch ready to receive the beautiful body of a siren, the glaucous scaly body.

Ermentrude took pleasure in contemplating the smooth brown rock, in the unconfessed hope of glimpsing there, one evening, the lassitude or languor of a siren lying on the wrack.

She mentioned it one day to an old man who was instructing her in the law of Myths.

"The sirens no longer sing," replied the old man, devoid of chimeras.

"Why don't they sing any longer?" asked Ermentride, with an ardent incredulity.

"Because the world has changed," said the disillusioned and veridical old man. "The world has become as gray as ash since those melodious times. And people have changed too; they're rebellious to all splendor. Today, the companions of the ingenious Ulysses would listen to the song of the Sirens without peril. The Sirens know that. That's why they no longer sing."

"Why do you say that the world has become as gray as ash?" asked Ermentrude, obstinately. "Isn't the sea that was the cradle of the Sirens still as fecund? Isn't it still beautiful, with its blue and black waves and its bright reflections of summer?"

She interrupted herself in order to follow with her eyes the aerial passage of a sail.

"The earth is, in fact, still the same, but the times and people have changed," sighed the old man, as he went away, curbed by the burden of old age.

Ermentrude meditated for a long time on what the veridical and disillusioned old man had said: *That's why people have changed . . . the world has become as gray as ash . . . the Sirens are no longer singing . . .*

She meditated for a long time in the darkness before going to sleep, in a sad slumber.

A blue moonbeam woke her up.

The rumor of the sea had become subtle and caressant. A perfume of iodine and algae came in through the open window. In the air, there was I know not what insidious promise. Space was vibrant with a glad expectation.

Ermentrude got up, attracted by that indefinable appeal, and went down to the beach, where the shingle was shining like broken crystal. She stopped before the waves, struck by an adoring stupor. The shiny and polished rock was gleaming like onyx and agate. A strange nocturnal radiance was reminiscent of a living pallor.

Was it the double illusion of the sea and the moon? Ermentrude thought that she could see a Siren, languidly extended, whiter than the frisson of the surf, who was laughing at the waves. Her hair was bathed by the water, like floating algae. Her glaucous scales were blue-tinted in the starlight. And her green and azure eyes reflected the double clarity of the sea and the moon.

Ermentrude remained motionless, in ecstasy. It seemed to her that her entire being was nothing more than a melodic tremor. The flux and reflux of harmonious blood was singing in her veins. She was happy, like a wave under light. Her entire being was no longer anything but an exaltation and a heroic symphony.

But a cloud veiled Selene's face obscurely . . . and the form whiter than a frisson of surf disappeared, as if it had plunged into the waves. The sea became opaque and heavy again. All the musical clarity was extinct.

Ermentrude launched a desperate appeal into space. Only the monotonous sobbing of the metallic waves responded to her. And from the depths of her memory, the words of the disillusioned old man returned:

"The Sirens no longer sing . . . for the world has changed . . . the world has become as gray as ash . . . the Sirens know that . . . that is why they no longer sing . . ."

For the first time, the child doubted her dream. For the first time, she sensed within herself an incredulous soul in revolt.

In a supreme surge toward the fugitive chimera, she plunged into the opaque and heavy sea. A metallic wave carried her away. She disappeared, the prey and victim of the Mediterranean, which was the cradle of the Sirens.

# THE LAST SIREN

## by Maurice Magre

"**B**EAUTIFUL flowers for your little friend . . ." said an old woman to Jean Noël, holding out a bouquet of roses.

And Jean Noël took the bouquet and gave it to his friend. As he put his hand into his pocket to pay the flower-seller he felt that the coin he took out was the last one. That coin was a golden louis. Jean Noël looked at it for a second; the setting sun made the metal shine with a gleam that seemed to our hero to be of inestimable beauty. He gave the coin to the old woman and thought:

*I've lived mindfully and without counting. Life has been a happy dream for me. And this is the supreme reality. For the last time, I shall shake the hand of Rosette, my mistress. I've consumed all my fortune; I've spent all the money that my friends and my father's friends were capable of lending me. Let's accomplish without sadness and without regret the sole gratuitous action that I can accomplish henceforth.*

"Let's go to dinner," said Rosette. "I'm very hungry."

Jean Noël smiled. Nearby there was an expensive restaurant where gypsies played violins and which was full of beautiful and elegant people.

116

"Go in there and wait for me," he said. "I need, this very instant, a volume of the history of philosophy that is at home, in order to elucidate a certain point, doubtful in my mind, regarding the life of Plato."

"Plato is insupportable," said Rosette. "Hurry up."

They separated. Rosette went into the restaurant. Night fell.

Jean Noël went down the Avenue de l'Opéra lightly, saluted the Théâtre Français and reached the Seine. A great rumor resounded. Trams with huge red and green eyes were circulating, screeching and huffing. The Institut extended its solemn shadow. Jean Noël had a moment of sadness on thinking that he would never be seated in that monument, as an old man. But he was consoled by the thought that Rosette would wait in vain all evening in the restaurant, and he would thus be avenged for her lies and deceits.

He had accustomed himself a long time ago to the idea of death. However, he hesitated between the Pont des Arts and the Pont Neuf. He finally chose the Pont des Arts, remembering that one summer day, a young woman passing over it with her mother had smiled at him. He reviewed that charming and disinterested memory and thought that, in sum, his life had been unexpected and happy.

The bridge was deserted. The black water was splashing down below and, meekly, he let himself fall.

There was a second of frightful anguish; confusedly, he heard a voice say: "How mad that man is!"

It was a fish that was passing by. Jean Noël struggled, thought inexplicably about the watch that he had in his waistcoat pocket, suddenly gripped by the urge to know the exact time, and then lost consciousness.

When he woke up, an exquisite music was resounding. It was a song, the song of a human voice, but a voice softer than any of those he had ever heard.

*Is it possible*, he thought, *that the fictions of religion are true? Am I in the paradise of Christians; am I going to see God the Father; is it the voice of the angels that I can hear? How can I be here, a man who doesn't believe in God and accomplished on earth a thousand sins in which I rejoiced?*

He opened his eyes, and his surprise was enormous. He was lying in a subterranean cave, on a bed of heaped-up fabrics, in the midst of objects of every sort, which rendered the place similar to both a museum and a brigand's lair. There were weapons, men's garments, sparkling jewels and chipped statues. And beside him, a woman of marvelous beauty was lying and singing.

She had put her arms around Jean Noël's neck, and he could feel the quivering of her skin. He could see that the skin in question was incomparably white and pleasant to the touch. Long blonde hair streamed like a delightful wave over our hero's face and hands.

He made a movement to get up, but then the woman stopped singing, the grip of her arms tightened, and Jean Noël felt upon his own lips the caress of two moist, profound lips that enabled him to know a kiss softer than all the kisses he had known on earth.

Shortly thereafter, when their embrace had relaxed, Jean Noël, full of astonishment, pleasure and bliss, spoke as follows:

"I certainly cannot believe that I have entered into the supernatural domain of death. I cannot imagine it so sweet. A purely terrestrial grace ornaments your face. But tell me, by means of what combination of circumstances, having thrown myself from the height of the Pont des Arts into the profound Seine, am I savoring your presence and your kisses in this unknown place?"

"That's men all over," she replied. "Always wanting to know! Thus, they kill a little of their happiness every day. Do I care about your name and your life? But no matter; you shall know everything. I'm the one who saved you as you were about to perish under the water, and who brought you here to my subterranean dwelling. I'm not a woman. Know that here, in the very heart of Paris, not far from the place you call the Louvre, a short distance from the temple of stone and iron full of strange monsters known as the Gare d'Orsay, the last of the sirens lives!"

As she spoke these words she drew aside the veil that covered her, and Jean Noël, stupefied, was able to see that half of her body was covered in scales and similar in form and color to that of a fish.

"All my companions have been dead for a long time. And I, the last of my race, have fled the sad modern seas and swum up this river, for the sight and the company of men has always been necessary to our life. Sirens are amorous; they need caresses and kisses. But since you have been traversing the waves in high iron ships, the tempests have been very rare that permitted me to hold a living mariner in my arms. When my last sister died, the solitude was too burdensome for me and I came here. I watch the drowned pass by with their glaucous eyes and their open arms.

"I see some who have been thrown involuntarily into the water with knives in their breasts. I see some who are lamentable and ugly, and excite my pity. There are the bodies of little children who have hardly seen the sun, and whose mothers have thrown them into the water immediately. Often, I've seen madmen throw themselves from the height of bridges, and I've been able, as I did for you, to collect them and save them. I've known their amour. They've told me their stories. There were gamblers, ambitious men, and beggars. There were lovers who were committing suicide because they had been abandoned by their mistresses. The kisses of those were the best; the bitterness of tears was mingled with them, as well as I know not what terrible ardor engendered by the desire to forget. I can say without pride that I've often consoled them for their chagrins . . ."

"I can easily believe that," replied Jean Noël.

"Once, there was a poet who read me his works. They caused me great tedium, for I heard no art in his words. His verses spoke of nothing but amour, and I saw with surprise, at the first kiss, that he was unfamiliar with it. But I educated him, and it was drunk on caresses that he left my dwelling . . ."

Jean Noël made a movement of surprise.

"I divine your thought," said the siren. "You're astonished that the poet of whom I'm speaking left my arms. You share the prejudices of your fellows regarding me and my race. You believe that we cause those we attract toward us to die. That is an unjust calumny; it is reported in the voyages of Ulysses by the old poet Homer. That storyteller, famous among you, was a liar. He slandered us because he was blind, because he could not contemplate us, and one detests the good things that one cannot enjoy. We are, on the contrary, good and compassionate, and I shall give you proof of it. Take from among my riches those that you desire; I'll take you out of this cave and out of the water, and you'll be free."

Full of joy, Jean Noël, to whom the proximity of death had rendered an appetite for life, thanked the siren effusively. He took a purse of gold and a precious ring, and exchanged a last kiss with the person who had saved him.

"Adieu," she said, "my lover of an hour. Be happy, but sometimes think, as you go along the bank of the river, that between the black waters and the screech of the locomotives, her senses burning with desire for beings of a different race, the last of the amorous sirens is wandering in the darkness."

A nocturnal wind was blowing. Jean Noël found himself back on the bank of the Seine. His garments were wet. He had a purse of gold in his pocket and a precious ring on his finger, made of a pearl similar to a teardrop.

*Was it a dream or a reality?* he wondered.

At a slow pace he went back to the restaurant, where Rosette was waiting for him. She was still there, a little anxious and very irritated, but he did not listen to her reproaches.

"I was delayed reading the life of Plato," he said.

It was midnight.

"That's too implausible. I've had a dream."

They went home. Rosette did not remain rancorous for long. She said to him: "I forgive you!" Then she kissed him and pressed herself against him.

But Jean Noël, having pushed her away for the first time, understood then that he had not had a dream, and that he had known the amour of the last siren.

# THE SIRENS

## by Pierre Mille

THERE is a man who has lived with the sirens. It's at Zeilah that one can see him now. He buys coffee from the caravans that come from Abyssinia and gives them in exchange old Maria-Theresa thalers, empty cartridge-cases, loaded cartridges and rapid-fire rifles that serve to kill Europeans. But many years ago he was the keeper of a lighthouse in the Farsan isles in the Red Sea, and that's how he saw the sirens.

He isn't mad. I assure you that I don't think he's in the least mad. Only he no longer speaks English very well because he spends most of his time, for his commerce, talking with the indigenes in Arabic or Galla, or Amharic, which is the language of the true Abyssinians, those of the mountains. And then, when he consents to relate his marvelous adventure, he sometimes interrupts himself for a long time, such a long time that one goes away without having the patience to wait for the end.

I don't know why he stops. Perhaps it's when he sees the sirens again more clearly . . . and for other motives, very mixed: because, for entire days, he did nothing but sleep or dream with them, on the rocks and in the hollow pools of warm water, and then, of those days when he was so happy, he retains the taste, because they were delectable, but he doesn't find anything to say, because they were empty, absolutely empty of action, while his heart was full; because he has secrets, also, things that he doesn't want to say, out of modesty, or for fear of not being believed; finally, out of jealous suspicion, because he's afraid that someone might go where he knows they are. I'll try, however, to recover his story in my memory. But you won't have, like me, the vision of his bright, moist, unfathomable eyes, the eyes that made me think of the abysms over which he claims to have floated for months.

He said:

You don't know what it's like to be the keeper of a beacon in the Farsan Isles. There's no sea more badly made than the Red Sea. One thinks that it's large, but that's only an appearance and an illusion. There's only one channel in the middle, deep but rather narrow, where one can pass through. The rest is full of banks of coral or extinct volcanoes, planted in the middle of the channel, the sole utility of which is to serve as reference points for mariners. The big ships head straight toward the volcanoes like moths attracted by a gas jet. The gas jet is the lighthouse. They call that reconnoitering.

And they come, one after another, screwing their twin propellers in waters warmed by the sun, stuffed with living things: jellyfish; starfish armored with stony lace; microscopic algae; and when they've seen, in day-light, the points of those arid pebbles, or, in the great night full of the even and dry wind from the deserts, with fires lit on the shores, they give a little turn of the wheel and they go away very quickly, seeming to say: "Is that you? We know now that we're on the right route, but you aren't pretty to look at, so good night!" Such is the ingratitude of those great machines.

It's never fun being a lighthouse keeper. But sup-posing that there are lighthouses in Hell, confided to the most compromised of the damned, those damned can't be much more unfortunate than the poor devils who nourish the red fires of the Red Sea. A cistern-boat came every month to bring me water and provisions; and when the crew detachment disembarked I started to laugh like a savage: "Men! Men! How oddly made men are!" Then they went away, and I remained alone with my matelot, a Danakil incapable of pronouncing three words of English.

There wasn't a single blade of grass or plaque of moss on that rock; nothing but old hardened cinders, pumice stones with veins of green and red lava; and the terrain, which sounded hollow under foot, was so hot that I sometimes said to the captain of the cistern-boat: "What if the volcano were to reawaken?"

He replied: "It's the sun, imbecile, that burns this pebble. The volcano is dead, quite dead!"

But the Danakil made grimaces in order to change the subject; all Danakils know that talking about things makes them come, and he was scared of the volcano.

One night—it was just after the boat had left—I seemed to respire an unexpected and yet familiar odor, an odor of chlorine, as rough as the one that catches you in the throat in big laundries. I dreamed, imagining that I was seeing the big vats full of lye, and the women leaning over the pale water, beaters in hand, their breasts gleaming with sweat over their open bodices. That gave me pleasure.

The Danakil, who was on watch at the lamp, came to take me by the hand in a fearful fashion. I opened the little window in my room and the same odor of chlorine nearly made me fall backwards. The entire island was fuming. Columns of noxious vapor were coming out of the ground in hundreds. They came out in gusts, gasps and hiccups, as thin as the clear thread of a lit cigarette, rising in enormous jets like the escape valve of a steamboat's engine. I went downstairs, I wanted to run—I was as naked as a worm because of the heat—toward one of those fumaroles.

The Danakil shook his head and said to me: "The water! The boiling water! It's eating the land."

I put my foot on the soil and pulled it back swiftly. The islet was dissolving under the subterranean pressure of acrid springs charged with chemical poisons, and boiling. It was dissolving like a sugar-lump; it was turning to mud, into stinking dirt, morsels of rock that were cascading down softened slopes, into bubbles full of gas that went "pfft" when they burst, dirty abscesses in that dirty ground. And the lighthouse started swaying like a tree, because it was being eaten away at the base, and now it could no more stand upright than a match on a pot of molten pitch.

I shouted to the Danakil: "To the sea, to the sea right away!"

I scalded my feet in that mud, which was burning and decomposing; I felt the bite of flames over my skin—black flames, if I can put it like that, for I never saw a spark in that stifling darkness—but finally, I reached the hospitable sea, the calm, fresh, maternal, welcoming water. She took me on her back.

The Danakil? I never saw him again.

It was when I came round that I saw the sirens, on another islet, further to the south, where they had doubtless taken me while I was unconscious. My head, out of the water, was resting on a cushion of wrack, and I was very frightened before those shifting bodies, larger than humans, brown and lustrous, all streaming. I imagined at first that they were sea-lions or manatees, and that currents had thrown me by chance on to a beach they frequented. But as I extended my arm I perceived, leaning over my head, at the slight sound I made, a head scarcely rounder than a man's, with hair—very long black hair divided in the middle by a parting, and eyes more tender than those of the most tender of women, which were speaking to me.

For it's necessary to say before anything else that for as long as I lived with the sirens, I always understood what was happening in their brains by virtue of that kind of silent language that was spoken not only by their profound eyes but I know not what emanation coming from their entire bodies. They also understood me, although less well. That's because I only thought by reasoning, and they scarcely had reason, but they had sentiments as numerous, as varied and as nuanced as my logic.

I say "*elles*" for the sirens, as one does for swallows, seamews and gazelles, but they're a species, they reproduce, they have males and females. The first one that approached me wasn't a male, and when I thought, in a semi-delirium: *I'm alive! I'm alive! Is someone going to do me harm, now that I've recommenced living?* I understood that the being who was there—an animal, a fay, or a particular species of savage human?—replied to me: "There's no need to be afraid; you're with us."

I felt her breath on my forehead and her two round breasts like those of a woman, posing on my chest, out of amity. It was only later that I perceived that my friend only had stumps of arms, terminating in flippers, and two other similar stumps instead of legs. She was only happy and lively in the light water; her rump bounded there like that of mares in long grass.

I astonished the sirens more than they astonished me. My repugnance at nourishing myself on the fish they brought me, and my preference for shellfish, even though the pulp was as raw as that of the fish, appeared risible to them. I disconcerted them again when I refused to drink sea water, but they took me to a spring that emerged at the level of the waves under a cliff, and when I drank from the hollow of my hand they admired me; my hands were always marvelous things for them.

I made them necklaces of seashells, coral and nacre, garlands of algae as yellow as gold—and the enormous moustached males with the air of warriors, covered in scars, wore them with as much pride as the siren-women. Often, when they were all ornamented, they held a ball in my honor. Oh, their backs, their rude and long tresses, the straight breasts of the women under their upright necks, the quivering of their bodies under the green water! They took me to their tournament; I was afraid and I screamed; but they carried me away like a child, with cares so gentle, in spite of their velocity, that I felt nothing but a bitter pleasure, a vertiginous sensuality.

One evening, they all sang.

Until then, I had only known them to use the mute language that I mentioned. Their song didn't have any words either, but every note said more than a long human discourse. That isn't a figure of speech; I distinguished the meaning of their lament as clearly as if it had been written on paper. They sang; there were dolorous cries, harmonious and slow, so sad and so clear in the mouths of the siren-women, so grave and somberly desperate in the profound throats of the males!

They sang about the antiquity of the race of sirens, and its decadence. It had appeared almost in the first ages of the world, when the sea covered the whole surface of the globe, and the sirens had been the first attempt of Nature to realize, in the womb of the universal ocean, a being that was not a pure brute, to create an organism that truly had a brain and a heart. And then the land had emerged from the waves, and Nature had abandoned that marine sketch. She had left it there, imperfect, even degrading in the course of the centuries, and the sirens have the sentiment of their ruinous grandeur and their decadence. We humans suffer eternally from being almost similar to God, of whom we have an idea; the sirens suffer from being almost similar to humans and not having conquered human intelligence.

They ought to have been monarchs of the ocean, as humans reign over the fields, the woods and the mountains, but Nature had forgotten to perfect them, and the sharks will soon have devoured the last of the sirens. That is why they once followed the hollow boats, drowning sailors put to sleep by their charms; it was out of jealousy. But now the race is going to die. There are only a few tribes of sirens in the Red Sea and on the other side of the world, on the edge of the Malay archipelago, and, far from drowning me, my sirens had saved my life in order to enjoy the melancholy pleasure of seeing a human at close range, a specimen of the species to which hazard or who knows what mysterious design has given the empire, while inflicting humiliation, defeat and agony on them.

It is thus that the race of sirens contemplates its fatal destiny, remaining full of mildness, generosity and also futile vigor, when it's necessary to fight against the monsters of the abyss; and far better than humans they know and savor beauty: the beauty of the sky, the air and the waters, the mysterious rhythms of the blood in the arteries and the quivering organs. But for the rest, they're animals.

Thus, the moment has come to tell you one more thing. Being animals, so long as the amorous season hasn't arrived, the male and female sirens live as chastely as children. They form innocent couples; they live two by two, playing, fishing, and going to the gardens of the sea to look at splendid mollusks, living and flowery anemones and luminous fish that brush streamers of seaweed. Their instinctive souls penetrate one another and are only one. My siren friend had adopted me in that fashion, and when she drew me over the waves, with my arm on her shoulder, I felt happy, purely and delectably, as I had never been with a woman. Her entire body quivered under my caressant hand; but when I wanted more, she didn't understand.

I didn't imagine what would happen at the moment of amours. I said to myself *Then, she'll love me as one loves on land.* I was mistaken. When the great season comes, the couples disunite. I don't like to recall it; I'm horrified!

I'm not a prude, but I'm horrified because I'm suffering. When they experience the frenzy of desire, the siren-women are no longer anything but animals, and the males become roaring brutes. They no longer choose. Everyone went with anyone. I saw them bounding, stuck together, in the foam, their monstrous stumps writhing to enlace or for battles; the sharp teeth of males—never the same male—bit the nape of my friend's neck, and her eyes, her brown eyes, whose grace and caress I loved, no longer gazed at me.

When her great amorous fury was somewhat appeased, then she swam toward me. She said: "What's the matter?"

I replied; "I hate you!"

And with all her body and with all her senses she asked me the cause of my hatred; she explained to me that she needed all those males, one for his strength, another for his prudence, and the young ones, all the young ones, for their dash and their courage. And it was necessary that it was thus. I went to hide my head in the rocks.

"Ah!" she said to me, finally, weeping. "You're a human and I'm a siren. You want all of me, but I can't belong to anyone. You want me to be yours alone, when I no longer belong to myself, but to the god of my race. We were wrong to keep you with us . . . O my friend, put your hand on my shoulder once more!"

I obeyed her, and we cleaved through the sea more rapidly than we had ever done. We swam all through one night and half a day, to arrive at a flat beach, below a mountain where eagles were flying.

"Here," she said, "you'll find men similar to you and women as you desire them; adieu!"

But I knew, before her departure, what the love of a siren is; I knew her! The sand was warm under our bodies, the color of the sky filled my eyes. I still have in my mouth the salty taste of hers. I shall always have it. One evening, perhaps, she'll come back. Or I'll go to her.

Such was the adventure of Elias Whitney, who now buys coffee from caravans

# A SIRENS' NEST

## by Paul Arène

"NO one knows exactly how sirens reproduce; you'd have to be cleverer than me to say!

"One thing that's certain, however, is that there are old ones, as wrinkled as witches, and young ones with their babies, who swim around and come to suckle at their breasts. Navigators have seen that.

"Of course, no one has ever seen males. Perhaps they live in the great depths, and in the manner of fish, without ever knowing their females, they only approach the shore in order to spawn."

Interested by that beginning, I sat down in a corner of the boat, half-embedded in the sand at the prow, momentarily transformed into a kitchen.

"First of all," my interlocutor continued, without interrupting himself, in order to pour the green wrasse and the Saint Peter's fish reserved for the bouillabaisse on to the fresh roundels of a large cork-oak platter like a bloody shield, "do you believe in sirens?"

"Do I believe in sirens? As much as you, Patron Marc. It's necessary that there must be something true in what people recount, since they continue to enable talk of them, and since our ancestors erected altars to them more than four thousand years ago."

"Four thousand years! You're joking."

"Not in the least. If fortune ever falls to me from the sky and I come to possess, that poet's dream, a yacht like Gordon Bennett or Rothschild, or even a simple tartan, I'll appoint you captain and we'll make a little voyage to Paestum together."

"Where the devil will you find that seaport?"

"My God! Only a few paces from here, beyond Naples, in Magna Graecia."

"And you'll show me sirens there?"

"I daren't guarantee it, but on that legendary shore, of which poets once sang, where the air was saturated with odors that made virgins swoon, and interminable fields of rose-bushes covered with flowers twice a year, but which is no more today than a feverish marsh populated by buffaloes and strewn with ruins, I'll show you, very close to a temple of Neptune, at the corner of a rampart made of enormous rough-hewn blocks, above the giant door, a bas-relief carved in the stone when neither Marseille nor Rome existed, and representing, Patron Marc, a siren picking a rose!"

Patron Marc suddenly dropped his knife; and, let it be said in all modesty, at first I thought he was hypnotized by the truly excessive amplitude of my speech.

A presumptuous error! Patron Marc, although literate in his fashion, is more attached to fundamentals than to vain curiosities of style.

"A siren picking a rose!" he exclaimed. "And that happened four thousand years ago? But then, it's like my story."

"What story?"

"Why, the story I had begun to tell, of course. Patience! Just give me to put few embers on the 'fugueiron' and I'll tell you the end, while keeping an eye on my bouillabaisse to make sure it doesn't boil over."

This, then, is Patron Marc's story, reproduced as faithfully as possible.

※

Since you believe in sirens, you won't be astonished to learn that, not long ago, a customs man making his round toward the point of the Red Rocks found an entire nest of them.

A nasty place, the Red Rocks. Although you have solid feet and although one can admire a superb horizon from their crest, I advise you never to go strolling there when the wind is blowing from the east. Nothing but bare, polished rocks, glittering with salt spat out by the waves, for the sea, however little she's irritated, pushes her spray that far.

Seen from the sea, on the other hand, you'd swear it's a land of fays.

Everywhere, there are holes, damp grottoes in the sheer wall of porphyry, and creeks everywhere filled with blue water, so narrow and so deep that when you look up, the sky appears to be a ribbon.

Each creek has, at the terminus, its little sandy beach, where a boat can land—a disposition naturally favorable to contraband.

It was in one of those creeks that, one moonlit evening, having heard voices and thinking he was about to pinch smugglers, the customs man, lying face down and creeping over the rocks, perceived the sirens from above. There were four of them, one already of a certain age, but still beautiful, who seemed to be the mother, and three others, of which the youngest was sulking, with her fists in her eyes, weeping or pretending to weep, as children do when scolded.

Her mother was, in fact, scolding her, reproaching her for having gone out into the water in broad daylight in spite of her prohibition, and for having played on the sand at the risk of seeing her scales tarnished by the hot sun.

"The sand is so warm and so soft," sighed the siren, "and then, I have a great desire to reach that blue flower growing up there in the fissure."

"A blue flower, a blue flower!" said the mother. "As if our submarine gardens didn't offer a crop, among the algae and the madrepores, of thousands of living flowers, nuanced with the richest colors, and which don't wither. Not to mention the danger to which one is exposed, in going imprudently to pick terrestrial flowers, of becoming like women and, one's virginity lost, being subjected to the brutal caresses of mortals!"

After which, perhaps for the hundredth time, for the sirens were yawning, she told them an old tale of times gone by, the adventure of a siren who, metamorphosed in that way, became an empress, loved and died, having respired a rose.

With the consequence that, from then on, the little siren no longer thought of anything else but one day respiring a rose, at the risk of loving and dying; and for his part, the customs man, who was a bold fellow, no longer thought about anything but the siren.

Every time that his service permitted, in all weathers and even by night, he returned to roam the shore. Only, perhaps because it was winter, the sirens didn't show themselves.

Then he had an idea: that of bringing a few baskets of earth to the hollow of the creek, in a spot sheltered from the wind, and constructing a little garden, such as customs men construct around their little houses.

Then he planted a rose bush, and when spring turned it green again and the branches generated flowers, one morning, next to his rose bush, he found a dainty naked woman, very blonde, with a rose in her hand, who seemed to be asleep.

Having recognized the siren, he wrapped her in the cloak of his uniform, and carried her into his cabin.

For a year they were happy. She acquired a taste for her new life, and didn't give the impression of languishing.

But after a year, to the day—or, to put it better, to the hour—as the customs man, after his morning tour of duty, was in the process of following the narrow path that crowned the height of the creeks, he imagined that he heard the sirens singing in the distance.

Then there was a plaintive cry of adieu and the sound of a body falling into the sea; and when he arrived home, he found the cabin empty.

The wrack of the bed was still warm; on the plank that served as a table, by way of a souvenir, a coral necklace had been left, with a few seashells and fine pearls linked by those tenacious silken threads that large mollusks use to bind themselves to their rock.

The customs man was unconsolable. It's said that he started drinking and came to a bad end.

"For, you see," Patron Marc concluded, "a siren always remains a siren; and, born for the perdition of men, however much love she might have for one, she always regrets the sea."

Now Patron Marc poured out his bouillabaisse.

But, insensible to the appetizing vapors rising from the saffroned slices, for a long moment I followed in my reverie that antique tradition, which, recognizable in spite of everything beneath its popular disguise, brought me in Provence, from beyond the azure of our Latin seas, a perfume of the roses of Paestum.

# THE INNOCENT SIREN

## by Remy de Gourmont

LIONEL PAPPE gazed at absurd old engravings scorned by the men of today, and he visited with joy the landscapes inscribed in pale ink on frail yellow paper.

His voyage took him to an utterly bare isle, the shore of which was strewn with bones that seemed to have been brought there by the waves, pebbles rolled by the anger of the waves and the irony of the winds. In spite of that ugliness and the soil devoid of trees, grass and moss, the isle was pleasant and easy on the eye, because of a roseate vapor that enveloped it with a charm and gave sad skulls the appearance of large dying flowers.

Having more than one country to travel, Lionel Pappe was about to turn the page, already distracted by another desire, when a concert of voices and violins rose from the shores of the bare and roseate isle. Perched on the rock, three beautiful birds with women's faces were singing in an unknown language about infinitely sweet things, and in the water, three ambiguous beings, women in the head and upper body, were accompanying on nacreous violins the amorous song of the three beautiful birds.

Recognizing the sirens, Lionel Pappe smiled with a great deal of disdain, and began to make a critique, aloud, of that vain performance. He recognized the siren-bird genre; Homer had mentioned them, and he had seen a portrait in the Louvre of those singular creatures, sculpted for the ornament of an obscure bas-relief.

"The others are the classic monsters . . . but why are they playing the violin? The violin is not archeological. I have made a very ridiculous voyage this morning.

"My child," Lionel Pappe repeated to a young woman who had entered discreetly, a big blonde schoolgirl with bright eyes, almost as beautiful as the pale images inscribed on the pale yellow paper, "I have made a very ridiculous voyage this morning."

And the good professor, as a prologue to his lesson, recounted his excursion to the sad and roseate island.

"Yes, you're truly a good professor, Monsieur Pappe; you teach me things that aren't written either in books or on papyrus, nor on metal or marble. So you've seen sirens playing the violin?"

"I've seen that," replied Lionel Pappe, "and although ridiculous, I deem it disquieting."

"Because it isn't archeological?"

"Indeed, because it isn't archeological."

"I suppose," said the big schoolgirl with the bright eyes, "that you've never been afraid of sirens?"

"Why would I be afraid of sirens?"

"Because they're women."

"And you think, my child, that I'm afraid of women?"

"You ought to be afraid of things that are illogical, and women are illogical. They play the violin inappropriately; for grave and archeological men, they're ridiculous—like your sirens."

Lionel Pappe was surprised to hear such a speech. He looked at his pupil and perceived that he had before him a big schoolgirl with bright eyes, who was shaking her long curly hair proudly, and whose bosom was lifted up anxiously by tempestuous waves that were swelling and did not know where they were going to break. He was a prudent man, although very much a dreamer, and since he had been giving lessons to young girls he had never had the spectacle of such a metamorphosis. He treated his pupils as pupils, and none had yet reared up like this, ingenuously admitting the covetousness of his sex—and truly, he was afraid.

Lowering his eyes, he said, slowly: "My child, we'll continue our reading. Act three, scene eight."

"Monsieur Pappe," said the big schoolgirl, as if she had not heard, "what color are violin strings? Red, aren't they?"

"Yes," replied Lionel Pappe, obligingly. "A beautiful crimson. Now . . ."

"A crimson as bloody as this, as brightly red against the whiteness of nacre?"

As she spoke, she had opened her bodice, showing a red line on her left breast, very bright, on which blood pearled when she applied her hand to it, in a tragic manner.

"Monsieur Pappe, I tried to kill myself yesterday. Amorous chagrin? Not at all. I'm virginal in body and heart and I don't desire any lips—and can you believe that if I desired lips, they would turn away from mine? If I'd had an amour or caprice I'd have satisfied it. No, I wanted to kill myself precisely because I had no amour, nor desire, and hardly any curiosity, so faint that it wasn't worth the trouble of taking my dress off—my absurd big schoolgirl's black dress, shiny on the hip because of the bag I take to school. I wanted to kill myself out of ennui, I wanted to kill myself out of disgust for the miserable life that is destined for me. I wanted to kill myself out of hatred for the imbecilic books that have been imposed on my poor virginal intelligence, out of horror for the mental humiliation in which the rules maintain me under their barbaric feet. I wanted to kill myself because I believed that I could only liberate myself by consenting to forfeit my very liberty, because I believed that my beauty could only be affirmed by giving itself as a slave to a master—and because I don't want to give myself to a master. To all, yes; to one alone, no! I wanted to kill myself, and I was a coward—like a woman! When I felt the sting of the blade, my hand weakened, the tip of the weapon lifted, drawing along the skin that it skimmed this crimson thread. I'd like the scar always to remain vivid and red; that will remind me eternally of the moment when death enabled me understand life. I want to live. I'm only a woman; metaphysics doesn't attain me; I'm outside the range of its arrows, and it seems to me that I'd understand very well if anyone wanted to inform my flesh."

With a hysterical laugh, leaning toward Lionel Pappe, she said: "That's the crimson thread that is the red string of the sirens' violin."

"Child," said Lionel Pappe, "why seek excuses for desire? Let your flesh sing like the sirens' violin; never reflect about yourself, or solid images, or life, or death—and never come back here, for you'd be ashamed, innocent siren, of the victim of your song of love."

But the siren wept, and Lionel Pappe knew that tears are as salty as the sea in which the sirens swim.

# THE LITTLE WOMAN OF THE SEA

## *by Camille Lemonnier*

A strange and sarcastic figure came on to the môle, one of those equivocal faces with bold eyes and mute laughter, who nudge you with an elbow and then propose to you mysteriously to take you to the tavern.

This one, no one knew; no one had seen him get out of a boat, and yet he must have arrived at the time when the last boats were filing through the pass between the red light and the green light.

So he came on to the môle, whistling, among the mariners who were gazing out to sea, and he examined the terraces of the distant dike. He had the short blue jacket and lumpy felt hat of sailors after a crossing. He was leaning his enormous wide open hand on an object that he was hiding in his bosom, and which appeared to move from time to time.

Then, one of the men who never ceased looking out to sea with gray, vague eyes, approached him and asked him what kind of animal he was carrying in that fashion. The stranger blew silently in his face a laugh that reeked of garlic and bear sausage, and then shrugged his shoulders, and waited for the first flood in the world to descend upon the môle.

The tables under the awnings of restaurants emptied out; after the midday meal, families came toward the sea to breathe sea saline air. It was the end of a promenade; from the jetty one could see porpoises playing, buoys dancing or trawlermen coming home. The wind also whipped up skirts, carried away hats and tousled hair; there was no lack of distractions.

In accordance with human anticipations, a few people initially took an interest in the color of the waves and afterwards, in little groups of white jackets and bright dresses; others, laughing, smoking and exchanging a few words that had no connection with the splendor of the sea, unfurled, simply because it was their habit to come on to the môle for a moment, because people before them had always done that.

And after a little while there was the nucleus of a crowd there.

They scarcely paid any attention, meanwhile, to the glowering figure that was squinting insolently at the ladies, and soon began to reveal to them by signs the presence of something unusual under his jacket. People were suspicious of that smoked and bearded individual with the crafty gestures.

He was still laughing soundlessly, his laughter similar to the foam of the waves dying on the beach, as if he were sure that, once caught by what he wanted to show them, they would no longer go away.

Now, with his free hand, he was caressing, under the thick wool of his jacket, the form of the hidden object, with the thick fingers of his other had were pressing against him. His head was also inclined. With his tanned and fleshy face to be directing beneath it, gently the smiles of a nurse at a doll—or perhaps he was pouring abominable oaths through the gap in his jacket, poisoned by garlic and sausage, like his laughter.

Then once, the slight moan of a child rose up, a sad plaint such as little sad cats also make. Yes, something in the mariner's bosom had vibrated at length a cry of wounded life, a very frail and yet superhuman dolor, which, on reflection, challenged the analogy with the child or young animal. It was more like a distant and frightened voice, like that of the wind in the mass during the nights of the equinox, such as a lighthouse-keeper hears in his little room, under the helpful fixity of his great lamp. Hou! Houhou! Houhouhou!

The poor fishermen who were on the môle knew that agonized voice well. More than one had heard it sobbing in the squall and then, signing themselves, they said together that it was mariners who had died in the abyss who were returning between two waves. They drew nearer; now, they were no longer looking at the sea before them, and holding their beards closed in their rude faces.

The hard fellow continued to laugh soundlessly with a cynical pleasure, as if, by laughing, he was certifying the joy of making a soul suffer somewhere.

He no longer had the same eyes; his proud gaze coruscated savagely like a black reef under the oblique crimson of the setting sun.

146

Again he leaned his taut muzzle over the gap in his jacket and was seen to make the one-handed gesture of touching the mysterious little thing. For the second time the unusual voice cried out, the little voice that caused a chill in the bones as if it had been heard before during a voyage at sea, or in another life, or in a dream.

Soon, the crowd flowed; it accumulated there, behind the sailors, those stupid or basely amused faces that participate simultaneously in the unconsciousness and ferocity of mobs. And ironic young men shouted: "Show us the toy! Let him show it if he doesn't want us to think that he's carrying a little living thing in his bosom!"

The fishermen, the poor people in surcoats and clogs, shook their heads; they were waiting patiently; they had already waited like that for days and nights for the return of boats, standing on the môle, their teeth clenched; and they knew full well that there was only a human being, a creature in distress, who could utter such a cry. Sometimes, it ceased for a short time. Then the large coarse hand touched it, and once again the voice rose up and rendered the mariners very pale.

Then the adventurer, with a theatrical gesture, threw his hat down at his feet. He gave the impression of a king with his coppery complexion, the curly astrakhan of his hair and his golden clapper-rings in his ears. He looked at the crowd scornfully. Now, in an idiom florid with the wrack and iodine of the most variously polyglot seas, he announced the incredible thing, and he pointed imperiously at his lumpy felt hat on the large paving stones of the môle.

A rain of coins fell. Ardent breaths surrounded him as, in procession, in the smoke of candles, he climbed up behind Mary's silvery robe, and it was the little people of the market stalls, the good people who had kept the humble faith.

This happened: the stranger took up his collection, stuffed it in his pockets, and looked at the crowd with a livid face; he was no longer laughing, his lips were trembling.

There was a great silence; then, one by one, the buttons of the reefer jacket were undone, and between the flannel shirt and the tattooed skin of the veteran, nestled in the warmth of the stomach, in the clumps of hair of the male breast, the head of a tiny woman appeared, with pale feverish eyes under thin filaments of green hair. There was also the suffering gentleness of a marmoset, the astonished and sad candor of a female seal pup emerging from a bowl before a public of soldiers and children, with a round smooth head that only lacks headbands.

Oh, most of all, it was a little jewel of flesh, as nacreous as a seashell, a living petrified foam with the hues of the most marvelous fish, and the entire prism, all the flowers of the gardens of the rainbow in the mirror of a lagoon on the edge of the sea. It was lightly clad in frippery of gold and silk, a piece of advertising cloth that had once shone on the shaking hips of an Asian dancer.

No one had any desire to laugh; rather, they were gripped by anxiety, a vague fear as before a prodigy, an elementary and abandoned form, before a trial that God had carried out in the first ages. And no arms, but little stumps or palmate fins, timid and frail apparatus that had, at that moment, the grace of an amorous gesture, on the two sides of the breasts, dainty breasts, pointed and pink, like the breasts of a tiny virgin Eve. The multicolored piece of cloth was then wrapped around something that could not be seen; one could not tell where there was a body for that minuscule bust, nor whether that body had legs.

And all of that living thing remained stuck to the breast of the man, with a charmed and suffering submission, by the nickel-plated links of a small chain, which was fixed at one of its ends to an unknown point of the hidden form, and on the other was attached to the ample triple turns of a red sash with which the clown with the face of a pirate had girded his loins.

The eyes, above all, were admirable, like lucid and sensitive enamels the color of aquamarine, sensible to the nostalgic emotions of a soul, the visible palpitations of a heart. One thought one was seeing boats bobbing, billowing sails on a bright marine morning.

The poor fishermen were not deceived; they had arrived at close range. With trembling mouths and ecstasy in their immense eyes, they leaned forward and looked under the jacket. They would not have looked differently at the holy presence of a relic. And they all kept silent, as one does at sea when the water becomes black and begins to splash under the hulls.

One, very old and a little feeble-minded, had taken off his bonnet and was praying. No one could have said why the man was praying. Eventually, another of the fishermen took a step forward and tried to touch the little pale flesh beneath her green hair. However, that one, no more than the poor men of faith who surrounded him, had no doubt; he advanced his hand with a devotional and timid gesture, and his entire body was trembling.

The murky face of the seaman went green, as if he were being tortured by colic, and immediately he uttered dire oaths in his baroque jargon. Now, very quickly, he closed his jacket, chewing obscure imprecations between his teeth, and under the anger of his fingers, like the wounded cry of a little Desdemona, the voice rose up. Then he picked up his felt hat, planted it across his temples with a furious blow of his fist, and already, with his shoulders, he was driving back the crowd, and rapidly reached the stairway at the extremity of the môle. Only a few witty young gentlemen insulted him from a distance.

The little old men of the boats, for their part, had put their hands in their pockets, the hearts suddenly cold, having sensed that a strange amorous force linked that diabolical navigator to that mysterious life, a force like the one that, for weeks, made them part of their boats and then brought them back there, to the môle, gazing before them, infinitely.

The sailor reappeared the following day, and then came back every day. No one, among the men of the port, would have been able to indicate which ship had disembarked him, nor from what country he had arrived. At the hour of the "good society" he camped himself on the large blue flagstones.

Now, with his cynical and malevolent laughter, he seemed to challenge the fishermen. They threw their sous into the felt hat alongside silver coins. And then the comrade, after having excited the little wounded cry by means of iterated pinches, thus biting public curiosity, or perhaps manifesting another sentiment that no one knew, undid the buttons of his jacket and exhibited the ball of pale flesh with the aquamarine eyes, the eyes like slow waves of life.

Immediately, those frightened eyes turned toward the sea, toward the plaint and the appeal of the great waters beyond the môle; it seemed that they were about to expire in a spasm, so fresh, so divine, like the orients of genesis, like the first mirrors in which life was reflected. Then, the adventurer tugged the chain violently and he obliged the poor eyes, like sick flowers, bleak and feeble sea-anemones, to turn toward the land.

In their turn, the men of the port, the mariners of the big ships and the long-distance fishermen, arrived to see the prodigy.

Always the clandestine individual clenched his teeth and eluded any response as soon as anyone interrogated him about the provenance of the little thing.

What did it matter to them? They loved her with a profound faith, as an idol, like a little virgin saint who had come to them on the crests of the waves. Old men affirmed that they had seen, playing in gold and silver nets, among the sifting of the stars, little women of the sea who had the same green hair. Somewhere at sea, where no boats went, there were mysterious isles where those daughters of the waters lived.

Oh, how nostalgically, in their wordless souls, they loved her and feared her, the little siren, surrounding themselves with signs of the cross as if for a sin, beside themselves at the same time with carnal and mystical fervor before her minuscule amorous breasts, palpitating with all the unknown of the sea; there were some who wept as they looked at her. There were some who went away singing songs.

Now the poor people of the boats were sure that the bumpkin, who trafficked her beauty and her dolor so vilely, exhausted upon her secret and wrathful ill-treatment. He too was caught by the roots by a damned amour, and he took his revenge; he whipped her, he stuck the anger of his fingernails through the gap in his jacket into her flesh, or he pulled her green hair with a horrible mute laugh. And then, oh, then, there was the lamentable cry, that cry like the screech of pulleys in the night of ports, like the sob of the wind around the window of the watcher in the tower of the lighthouse. That was what simple hearts said to one another.

Now, toward the time of the equinox, the north-wester began to blow a tempest; the entire sea came over the môle, and in the evenings, they went, hands in pockets, to the end of the main street to see whether the boats that had set forth might have come back.

The man, expelled from the môle, also came to that place; he sheltered under a porch, and once again they stopped gazing at the sea. There was another cry now, a shrill cry that never ended, like that of a madwoman. Her master could scarcely retain her; she made efforts to launch herself toward the sea.

Then they recommenced their signs of the cross, for they had heard that voice before. Always, boats sank when that frightful voice cried like that. Her eyes also had a strange and supernatural beauty that vibrated, which agitated like the needle of the compass. A magnetism granted her the pulse of the tempest.

Then the great anger of the waves died down. She remained quite dead for three days, her eyes troubled and livid. And the sinister pirate pinched her in vain, she no longer cried out.

One day, as he had drunk more gin than was reasonable, he fell asleep on the blue flagstones; he nursed the petulant alcohol there for a long time. Suddenly, the port heard frightful clamors; the men of the boats came running and perceived him eating his hands, rolling on his belly like someone seized by *grand mal*.

Then a great pain came to them all; perhaps the little woman of the sea had gone; and they searched for her everywhere toward the water.

He threw himself upon them now, swearing and laughing; they did not defend themselves and considered him with sad and resigned eyes.

Time went by; he spent entire days sitting on the môle; no one knew what he was looking at out at sea, with his eyes fixed corroded by the salt. Sometimes he bellowed like a sperm whale, like the siren of a ship in distress, or, very softly, nodding his head, he prolonged the plaintive wail of a sick child.

And the fishermen had remarked that he too, at the approach of a tempest, now uttered shrill cries. At high tide, when the water began to climb over the môle, one of them took him by the arm and brought him back to the port, where he walked, his eyes sharp and straight, always hugging something against him that made him laugh, with his soundless laughter.

One winter night, the sea growled so terribly that the shepherds in the dunes a full league from the coast thought that it was arriving and fled into the country. The mariner was never seen again. It was supposed that he had heard a voice and had gone out there, from which the little woman with the green hair had never returned.

# THE LAST SIREN

## *by Lucie Delarue-Mardrus*

NO one spoke the delightful name of the people who had died in the abandoned property, the grand old gardens of which went all the way down to the sea. For decades no one had passed that way any longer. But perhaps *something* passed that way? The sea, which has so many stories to tell, doubtless wrote this one in the sand of the little creek with the tips of her waves, which left secret white traces behind every day when the tide ebbed. But whether the beds of wrack sometimes remained hollowed out at low tide, as if haunches had rested there, no one would ever know. The dramas of an absolutely solitary tiny terrestrial and marine area did not concern anyone in the world.

A day came when the property was bought. The house was horribly renovated, the gardens turned over and shaped; nothing more remained of the abandon slowly amassed among those things like an unknown treasure. That real being, a monsieur, came to sit down, banal and content, in the midst of the past, and his family, around him, broke all that silence with the noise of human life.

One of his first cares was to descend alone to the creek, with the intention of fishing with a net. He was having a house-warming party the following day and he wanted something caught with his own hand to fry for the morning meal he was giving his friends.

He was seen, red-faced and amused, his feet bare, advancing toward the retreating sea. His large net, disposed over a wooden square, was weighing upon his shoulder at the end of a long pole. The light of the setting sun splashed the sand, the mud and the pools around him. The world glistened at his feet like Chinese lacquer. At sea, the sun was dying. He was dreaming of little soles, dabs, plaice and shrimp. He searched for a nice hole of troubled water, and found one: a hole as large as a pool; in truth, as wide and deep as the pools of important persons of old.

Suddenly, turning crimson, the man stared with eyes bulging from his head, because he had just thrown his net effortfully and saw it filled to breaking point by a long scaly body, the frantic lashing of whose tail shook his arms terribly. But did he not also divine, caught in algae, mesh and hair, a human face whose frightened pale eyes were looking him? Were there not two little hands clenching and struggling?

He made a movement to flee, but pulled himself together very quickly, because marvels never astonish ordinary people, and such an adorably terrifying thing as finding a siren in his shrimp-net cannot disturb for long a monsieur who is fishing for a fry-up, without thinking about anything else. He only exclaimed: "What a funny eel!"

He would have been more charmed by an encounter with one of those mussel-fishers whose complaisant bosom one could evaluate from the corner of an eye, than the sight of a fabulous creature, frightened, wet and gilded.

That is why he only uttered a loud burst of laughter when the siren spoke.

"I was afraid of you," she said, "and yet I waited for you. You're the charming human that my mother saw from afar wandering at the end of the gardens, and whom she told me so much about when she died, when I was still as small as a gurnard."

Her head was raised. Drops of water were still streaming over her livid cheeks, all the way to her crimson mouth. Her nostrils were palpitating like the delicate gills of a fish. When she moved she spread a strong perfume of iodine and salt. In addition, the sea had ornamented her. Her hair was still extended by the seaweed that was mingled with it; her forehead was coiffed with starfish, and a few pearls were nested in the complicated hollows of her ears. Necklaces of seashells and coral were sliding around her neck.

But was not the most beautiful of those ornaments, displayed between the breasts imprisoned in the threads of the net, the luminous violet flesh of a jellyfish, like an unexpected item of glassware?

She could not free her hands. She repeated: "I waited for you."

As he did not say anything, she considered him at length with her immense eyes the color of water, in which the patch of the pupil flowered like a black nenuphar.

"You see," she said, "your fishing-trip, this evening, is a cast of the net of destiny. For such a long time I've been coming at low tide to lie in this bed, in order to watch for you. Soft and floating wrack carpet the bottom, and I often go to sleep here, my head in my arms, by virtue of gazing toward the land without seeing anyone come. Sometimes I risk myself at the very edge of the waves and, crawling over the mud and the sand, I drag myself to the shingle of the shore, in spite of my precious body being wounded by it. I stretch myself out on the wrack, still moist, and I gaze at the shining sun. I've even dared to sing to appeal to you. Do you know that no one in the world has yet known the taste of the oyster of my mouth? Why didn't you come? But now you've found me, and I shall no longer utter my great cry of appeal along the strand. You'll lie beside me in my bed and we'll espouse one another in the shifting submerged shadow of algae. And I, the last of my race, will give birth in my turn, as my mother did, and thus, the sirens of the sea won't die forever with me. Don't you see how richly I've arrived for you from the depths, streaming with maritime ornaments? The waves dress me with a robe of light, and I'm drawing behind me the entire sea for a mantle. Come! I am your nuptial siren, your wife, O king of lovers!"

The poor man pointed a finger at the changing scales and sniggered.

"What do you take me for?"

But the salty lady did not understand. She displayed the blue perplexity of her eyes to him. "Listen to me! Listen to me! Doubtless you don't yet know the marine secrets; but I'll teach them to you. Think that I'm alone, to populate the sea. Can I not know it entirely, I who only have its waves for companions? It is the waves that have rounded my breasts like the shingle that they roll. It is the waves that have deposited these pearls in my ears. They love me. I lie down softly in them, and it is for having cradled my body that they arrive so hollow on your shore. They have told me everything. I know the days of calm in which their glaucous and succinct skin barely swells, and the days of tempest when, black with storms and white with foam, they run in furious folly to charge the cliffs terribly. I know exactly the meaning of the changing sea, warlike and retractile. Its monstrous rumor is in my blood. I have seen its ripping rocks at close range, but I have also known long slumbers in its saline puddles, amid a little sand, mud and shingle, between a few shellfish and algae, and also profoundly drowned repose, when strange fish come to look at me with all their phosphoric soul, and the scales of my tail shine like gold in the silent obscurity. I've known the spring mornings when young women throw a few flowers into the bitterness of the sea, a few flowers to sweeten the sea, and the electric evenings of summer when boats draw a fiery wake behind them. I know everything! I'll teach you everything! Like me you'll understand the abyss and the surface, and the great evenings in the open sea when the acute dolor of seaweeds streaks the sky and my hairy head, cleaving the immensity, emerges in the sunset, in order for me to extend insensate arms toward the horizons of flame and desire, in the utmost depths of my being, to drink the sea and eat the sun!"

She had finally disengaged her little hands, which she raised above her head, her mouth wide open, her eyes turned to black.

And the man suddenly cried: "But it's true that she has breasts!"

Then, his hands forward, with a happy smile, he advanced toward the siren, and his two large palms were plastered in a single thrust upon the firm and streaming bosom.

She uttered a great chromatic clamor, like that of steamers in distress. Her entire body writhed in indignation, and in a moist frisson, turning round against him, she suddenly dug her ten fingernails into the ruddy cheeks, while, with a sweep of her furious tail, she pricked his legs with all her defensive spines.

Blinded, frightened, washed by the algae and the tresses, wounded by the fingernails and the spines, he was nevertheless able to seize her by the shoulders. She writhed in his fingers, struggled amid the gleams; but with an effort, he caused her to tumble back into the mesh, which he closed with an abrupt movement. Then, dragging her behind him furiously, he returned with long strides to the darkened strand, howling and still trembling with fear:

"You're nothing but a fish, after all! To the cooking-pot! To the cooking-pot!"

And his coarse laughter, through the rising marine night, drowned out the unusual cry that the last siren, as she died, directed toward the sea, and liberty.

# THE MAN OF THE SEA

## *by Arnold Mortier*

IT was in Dresden two or three years ago.

A friend of the signatory of these lines, passing through the capital of the kingdom of Saxe, was in a shop of comestibles where he was purchasing a few provisions for the journey. The service was slow, the packaging careful. Slightly fatigued, he sat down next to the counter and, while the merchant was arranging ham and sausages in a small basket, his eyes fell on some old sheets of manuscript, doubtless destined to wrap the greasy acquisitions of clients.

One of them was torn in half, the truncated phrases of which he tried to reconstitute:

> *What he had perceived in the waves was . . .*
> *. . . a Parisien, a Vien . . .*
> *. . . an inhabitant of . . . Dresden flee . . .*
> *. . . It was a bath . . .*
> *. . . a naked . . .*
> *. . . tracing a pink . . .*
> *. . . in the somber sea . . .*
> *. . . What . . .*
> *. . . satanic, what redoubtable spe . . .*

Other sheets lay scattered among various pieces of meat. He scanned them, and the reading interested him enormously.

"Where did you get these manuscripts?" my friend asked the shopkeeper.

"In truth," the fellow replied, rather astonished, "they've been in the house for a long time; a musician who came to lodge here with my grandfather in 1813 left precipitately one day, only leaving to settle his rent a trunk full of papers. The musician having never come back, we conserved those scribbles, father and son, until the moment when I decided to utilize them in this fashion. There were a large number of them, but those you see there are all that remain."

My friend easily obtained from the typical Teuton the gift of those few yellowing sheets "which aren't even worth as much as printed paper for making good bags," and, having returned to his lodgings he started rereading the German text, of which the rats had nibbled their share, and which time had rendered almost indecipherable.

The more he studied the semi-effaced lines, the more he was struck by the strange and quasi-symbolic form that he discovered in them. He repeated to himself obstinately: "One might think it an unpublished tale by Hoffmann."

Evidently, nothing permitted the supposition that the disorderly and ever-needy author of *The Cremona Violin* had neglected to have a single one of his literary and philosophical fantasies published; but my friend gave himself excellent reasons nevertheless and ended up, for want of material evidence, bringing together a series of probabilities that appeared to him to be conclusive.

After having observed first of all that the manuscript must be a copy, since it did not resemble known autographs of Hoffmann, he recalled very appropriately that the celebrated author of the fantastic tales had been brought, by the hazards of a more than agitated life, to occupy in Dresden the much sought-after post of the leader of the orchestra of the National Opera. That happened in 1813.

Now, it was the same year, 1813, that Napoléon entered Dresden.

The arrival of the victor of Lützen and Bautzen must have had, as a consequence, the precipitate flight of the German writer who, apart from his great literary and musical value, possessed a talent for drawing that had permitted him to publish bloody caricatures of Napoléon. The great captain, very sensible to attainments of ridicule, would certainly not have spared their author.

It then became explicable how Hoffmann had come to hide, probably under a false name, in the home of a local pork-butcher, and how he had departed suddenly without even having the time to take the unknown works, of which the tale in question must be the sole recoverable relic.

For want of the illustrious Xavier Marmier, who has so faithfully rendered into French the literary baggage of the great German storyteller, my friend was forced to furnish me with a very conventional translation of the text reconstituted by him. It is that translation that I am reproducing here without further commentary.

＊

Nature, which has multiplied on the coasts of Norway the gigantic cliffs crowned with pines, has not shown herself anywhere more fantastic and more picturesque than in the splendid bay of Vaagen, in the depths of which the white and red houses of Bergen appear.

It was on the occidental point of the bay that a jagged rock eroded by the sea was found, posed as if on a pedestal of seaweed and wrack, but covered nevertheless by mosses and evergreen trees, where Christian Vogt loved to come to dream.

Few human beings are as rudely tempered as Christian was for the struggles of life. An elevated noble and virile soul in a body of steel, an extraordinary intelligence developed by sane and forceful studies, he was entirely out of place in Bergen, in the midst of a busy population of fishermen and mariners, and fat merchants whose life was spent behind a counter or astride a barrel. He avoided worldly seductions, never frequented taverns, and seemed to be reserving himself for some great unknown task. He was the kind of man of which celebrated heroes and benefactors of humanity are made, and who become the instruments of destiny when destiny condescends to make them its plaything.

Christian was taciturn, not because he was misanthropic, but because he saw nothing around him but futile minds; apart from the old priest who, before dying, had had time to make of him a man of courage and knowledge, he never found anyone to whom he could talk, or who could respond to him.

God had isolated him on earth, first by rendering him an orphan in his early years and then by attributing to him a total of superiorities that so many other men lacked.

Every day, when the sun was already in decline over the horizon, Christian came to contemplate the immense infinity of the ocean from the height of the cliff of the promontory, which the mysterious work of the centuries had erected like a fantastic sentinel at the entrance to the bay of Vaagen.

In his mute and mystical observation, in his sublime and profound meditation, Christian was never alone. He believed that he was living in the midst of an un-known world, surrounded by supernatural spirits who understood his thoughts, his dreams, and his vague and as yet undetermined ambition.

One day, lending his ear to the muted chant of the ocean and seeking to imagine what the distant horizon was not showing him, he had just cried out with a noble impatience: "What can I do that is great?"

His attention was drawn to the foot of the cliff by a slight splash that, in spite of its lack of intensity, made itself heard in the midst of the more imposing sounds of waves breaking against the rock.

Christian leaned over, looking down below, uttered an inexpressible cry, got up with one bound and fled without looking back.

What he had perceived in the waves would not have made a Parisian, an inhabitant of Vienna or Dresden flee.

It was a bather, a naked woman, tracing a pink fur-row through the somber sea.

What a satanic dazzlement, what a redoubtable spell for that chaste and robust man!

The sight of the body with the voluptuous contours maddened him, and the smile of the pretty swimmer remained engraved in his eyes and in his heart; for, in spite of the rapidity of his retreat, he had had time to see that the woman was smiling at him. She had smiled at him, in fact, blissfully, immodestly, without embarrassment and without any apparent concern for her improbable nudity.

The next day, Christian did not come back.

He shut himself away, entrenched in a vain and sterile meditation, thinking even so and against his will about the apparition of the previous day.

That apparition was reproduced in a dream, and the awakening seemed full of shame.

Christian understood that retreat could only add to the obsession, while the great horizons that were familiar to him might perhaps deflect the course of his ideas.

In any case, the bather could only have come to that almost inaccessible place by chance. She certainly would not reappear there; he would never see her again.

And he returned to the cliff, full of assurance. The sea was calm. The waves were dying slowly at the foot of the rock.

Christian remained plunged in an anxious reverie. She was no longer there. That was what he had hoped, but he was surprised to regret the accomplishment of his hope. After a little while, however, he heard a slight splash and he saw again the beautiful body to which the fluidity of the sea in which it was playing scarcely lent a silvery gauze.

Christian was no longer afraid now.

Far from fleeing, he contemplated the perfidious spectacle and abandoned himself to unknown sensations.

On his knees at the edge of the cliff, in the posture that he had only ever adopted in order to elevate his soul toward God, he looked down—a man who had always wanted to look too high! He gazed, with a superstitious joy that he no longer tried to dissimulate, at that marvelously beautiful woman, whose smile gradually intoxicated him.

It was strangely lascivious, that smile, calm, incessant and as if fixed to the vermilion lips of the admirable creature.

Vanquished and fascinated, Christian wanted to get closer to the unknown woman; like a fanatical Hindu who slips into the temple by night in order to see the divinity, he would take advantage of the declining daylight to descend without being seen, he thought, and surprise her at his ease.

The enterprise was rude and perilous, the cliff being sheer and rather high, but Christian was strong and adroit. Furthermore, his natural vigor was multiplied tenfold by a truly unusual overexcitement, which metamorphosed him in his own eyes.

Twenty times, on the improvised route in the midst of rocks ready to fall away, he was nearly dragged down. He resisted everything and continued his terrible descent even so.

The sinuosities that he was constrained to follow grew increasingly steep and caused him in the end to lose sight of the sea, and the bather, and the smile that attracted him.

When he finally found himself on the strand, at the angle of a colossal rock, the unknown woman had disappeared.

Where was she? There was no trace, no vestige on the shore.

Where had she come from, then, via the high sea?

Poor Christian went home timidly, searching in vain for the key to the enigma.

For two more days, the two following days, he saw the pretty bather again in the same circumstances, and recommenced the same descent, with the same lack of success.

On the third day, he sat on the strand and waited. For certainly, if he were not the victim of some diabolical mirage, the mysterious creature would come back, and nothing could frighten her or put her to flight, since instead of the descent along the rock face, as on the other days, he would be there, at the moment of her arrival, very close to her, close enough to speak to her, and even to reach her.

Night fell, warm and starry. Christian did not sleep. He counted the hours, lending his ear to the distant carillons of Bergen, impatient and feverish, saluting with a cry of joy the first light of the rising sun. Would he see her again? From which direction would she come? Would she arrive in the bay from the open sea, or would she surge forth abruptly from behind a rock?

The wait was long. The hours of the day flew by without him being able to discover anything on the surface of the waves but the rapid flight of gulls, full of undulations and the inflated sails of fishing boats. He felt despair invading his soul; then everything was forgotten before the sudden vision of the beautiful swimmer. She was there, a few meters from the shore, and he did not even try to explain her sudden and supernatural appearance. He devoured her with his eyes, intoxicated himself on the sight of her. And she was still smiling.

She approached the shore, darting a strange gaze at him, fixed, troubling and unsustainable; then, suddenly, she described a semicircle and drew away, as if to reach the open sea.

Christian was an exceptional swimmer. He threw himself into the water with the impetuosity of young charger launched on an endless trail.

In a few moments he had caught up with the unknown beauty, who was swimming with a sustained and regular rapidity, not seeming disposed to do anything whatsoever to abridge or complicate the difficulties of his nautical course. When he arrived beside her she neither relented nor accelerated her speed.

She did not make any gesture of surprise, nor let any exclamation of joy or terror escape; she smiled—that was all.

He remained silent, content to admire her and not daring to speak to her. But that mute contemplation could not last. The passion of the young man, stimulated by the sight of that marvelous immodest body, was soon exhaled in ardent confessions.

"I love you! I adore you!" he said, with each stroke that carried them into the immense ocean . . .

She did not reply; she smiled.

"Respond to me, adored darling," he sighed.

She continued smiling.

"I love you!" he repeated, with a rage of obstinacy.

But there was always nothing but the eternal smile.

The day declined. Already, they had both been swimming for a long time, unrelentingly, without a rest, and without even changing the monotonous regularity of their movements.

How far would she take him?

She did not seem to experience any lassitude.

The young man, on the contrary, felt fatigued; he was maintaining himself by means of painful jerks, and he darted a long glance behind him.

A grandiose and imposing spectacle!

It was the hour when the setting sun modifies at every second the multiple coloration of the sea. The sheet of water traveled seemed immense. He could scarcely see the first reefs blanched by the waves. As for his favorite rock, he perceived it, confused, indecisive and imperceptible, as if surrounded by a sinister vapor. The promontory was no more than a pin-head, and Christian told himself that it had been sufficient for him to follow that silent and admirable creature for everything that he had believed to be large to appear to him very small.

However, his strength was exhausted. Every new wave seemed only to be coming toward him in order to engulf him in the vast ocean, the depth of which he sensed augmenting as he lost sight of the land.

He appealed to the woman to help him. She did not even appear to hear him, continuing to smile. That was too much. He succeeded in reaching her, by means of a supreme effort, and tried to seize her, mingling the voluptuousness of the first touch with the reckless grasp of a drowning man. But his hands only encountered icy arms, and shoulders over which they slid.

At the same time it seemed to him that beneath him, an abyss was hollowed out; the sea opened up and everything began to whirl. He thought that he had been transformed into a top, so rapidly was he spinning. The clouds in the sky were spinning too, and the big waves were spinning, sucking him in, drawing him into a gigantic funnel. Crabs of colossal dimensions were climbing along his legs, tickling the soles of his feet, which gigantic octopodes enlaced him with their tentacles.

All the monsters of the sea attacked his body, in order to drag him to the bottom. He wanted to scream, but the water closed his mouth. He saw, above him, in the vapors of the twilight, horrible heads that were laughing at his agony; in the foam of waves, huge phantoms extended arms to him; then the water closed his eyes. Then he heard again, in a muted roar, yapping voices that cried: "You're ours! You belong to us forever!" At that moment, the water closed his ears. At the same time as the great and eternal silence commenced for him, he clung to the beloved creature in a final convulsion.

Dominating the sound of the waves, a strange cracking sound was immediately produced, something like the mechanism of a clock breaking.

The man and the woman sank; the water seethed for a few moments.

The following day, in the depths of the bay, the tide washed up two bodies, tightly enlaced; one was the lacerated cadaver of Christian Vogt; the other was a mechanical woman, an automaton whose mainspring had broken.

The man's face expressed the tortures of a treble agony.

The woman was smiling.

The man was buried and the woman was repaired.

She will always smile, for the smile of dolls is eternal—like evil.

# THE FISHER OF MEN

## by Camille Mauclair

MONSIEUR LE COMMISSAIRE CENTRAL I am going to tell you exactly what happened, or at least what I know, about the disappearance of my poor comrade Legludic. I don't believe that I've merited blame in that sad affair. For ten years I, Yves Perreuc, have been in the coastal customs, for four years as a sous-brigadier; I have the Tonkin medal and the Sudan medal, two wounds, a citation in the orders of the day for the affair at Rac-Ninh, a proposition for a life-saving medal because of a gentleman bather whom I virtually pulled out of the water at Villerville, and not one bad mark in my entire service—in consequence, I don't pass for a liar.

However, what happened to me isn't ordinary, and there's only me who saw it. When I say that there was only me, that's only a manner of speaking, unfortunately there was Legludic, but now he's drowned, poor devil, without me being able to do anything about it. So I'm going to tell you what happened, exactly as it came about, and you can get what you can out of it, because you're a learned man; for myself, I still don't understand it very well, and if it were anyone else but me, I wouldn't believe what he said. Not only am I distressed to see a brave fellow dead, whom I'll miss, but I can't sleep any more at the idea that there's something under what I've seen that I can't explain. In brief, here's my statement.

It was seven o'clock in the evening. Legludic and I had just got back to our hut. He'd finished his day sooner than he thought; he arrived with a cunning expression.

"Yes," he says to me, "I believe there's a good opportunity for a man to distinguish himself today. Perhaps I can also earn my sous-brigadier's stripes."

It's necessary to tell you the both Legludic and I are from Port Navalo, that we go together like two fingers of the same hand, and that, in spite of my rank—outside of the service, of course—I talk to him like my brother . . . presumably, because I never had one.

I start to laugh and I say to him: "What have you dug up, Pierre?"

He replies: "I believe we can pinch, at the bottom of the cliff, in the little creek, the dirty fellows who've enraged us so much—you know, the types who passed tobacco and rum under our noses a month ago, one evening when you couldn't see three paces ahead of you. I've got something on them; it might be useful. Shall we go down right away? It's the time; we'll break bread when we come back."

I reply "All right." I pick up my utensils—for I'd already started to make the soup—and we take our jackets and rifles. It was beginning to rain a little but we can still see quite clearly and the sea wasn't bad. The tide was about to come in. We made fifteen hundred paces or hereabouts quite briskly and we slipped on to the sand and shingle all the way to a corner of the little cove.

There, Legludic says to me: "We won't have to wait long, and we'll catch them as if in a net, old . . ." At that moment, he shudders and whispers to me: "Are they early?"

I hear laughter. We advance into the rocks, one to the right and the other to the left, and suddenly I hear Legludic exclaim: "Oh! Well!"

I rejoin him in two bounds, and I see him standing, like a simpleton, in front of a naked woman—a stark naked woman, Monsieur le Commissaire Central. A pretty person, plump, blonde, with beautiful long bright hair that covered her back, a funny figure, green eyes, a bizarre laugh. She didn't seem to be embarrassed at all; she laughed as much as she could as she looked at us. She had more the air of a madwoman than a brazen one; at least, that was my impression.

Anyway, Legludic looks at me, vexed.

I advance and say: "It's forbidden to bathe like that, Madame. It's indecent. It's your fault if we've seen you, while doing our service; it's necessary to get a grip on yourself."

With that, we're about to turn our backs in order to let the person put her chemise on, when she lets out a burst of shrill laughter—I can still hear it—and we see her, far from being embarrassed, lying on the sand, her arms crossed behind her head.

Suddenly, I get angry and I say: "There's a story! It's necessary for you not to mock agents of the state, Madame. Contraventions of public decency are the affair of the gendarmerie, but all the same, you can't do that. For a start, where are your clothes?"

The woman laughed without responding. Legludic was very red. I was getting more and more annoyed. I said in a low voice to Legludic: "I'm no prude, old man, and I've seen a lot in the colonies, but this whore is too audacious. You've brought me to flush out the prey: I think that one's worth no more."

"Old man," Legludic whispers to me, "she's rudely beautiful."

And I see a sort of drunkenness in the eyes of the old dog. Monsieur le Commissaire Central, I say things as they are, and I swear to you that we were cold, hungry and had the intention of doing our duty. The fact is that the creature was a beauty. I've seen nothing like her. Her body was so white that it was like a light among the rocks. And, well, we're men like everyone, and I understood Legludic. But me, I only wanted the good of the service, and then, that woman's laugh sent a chill down my back and rendered me furious without me knowing why.

I raise my voice and say: "Will you answer me, yes or no? Where are your clothes?"

She seems to reflect, and says to me in a soft voice: "I . . . I don't understand."

"You don't understand? Where do you come from?"

She points at the sea.

"You've come from there? You've come by sea? Listen, are you making fun of us? We'll see. Why are you here, stark naked? Do you think that's any way to behave?"

She replies to me, still in a musical voice: "Stark naked? I don't understand."

"You? Come on, let's see, are we naked, the two of us? Is anyone naked?"

"I've always been like this."

"And you don't know that there are regulations, that it's disgusting to go about stark naked? That was done in ancient times, but now people are decent, and you don't date back to antiquity, my little lady."

She smiled, stretched herself and said: "I've always been like this."

Then I stopped being annoyed and I said to Legludic: "We'll let her go. Only we'll pass her over to the gendarmerie, you understand. What an affair! As for your bad lads, we'll pick them up another day. You must have been given false information, and as the time we've been talking to his crackpot has revealed us on the beach, they've had time to see us from a distance. It's spoiled. Let's go. One last time Madame, will you fetch your clothes from I don't know where, and go? No? You want to take a bath in the rising tide? Good. The brigadier at the gendarmerie will arrange it."

I depart into the rocks. Legludic follows me, reluctantly, and I grumble all the time, along the dune. I can still hear that creature's laughter. She seems so casual that one might have thought that she really lived in the water, that she was half fish. However, she had a body like all women, and if she was mad, it was in such a peaceful fashion! Monsieur le Commissaire Central, I ought to say that she gave the impression, above all, of a foreigner, someone who had come from extremely far away, and like the origin of the world: one of those animals that there are at the bottom of the sea, which have never yet been fished up . . .

In sum, I can't explain myself, but really, one might have thought that she was at home, that she had come out of the water and that she had always lived there. However, she had the body of a twenty-year-old.

What did you say? Do I know what a siren is? A tugboat's whistle? Oh, no, Monsieur le Commissaire Central, I don't know what you mean. Are there women of that sort? You say that they've only ever existed in fables? Anyway, all that I can say is that this one existed for real.

To get back to my deposition, when we got back to our cabin I said the Legludic: "We'll eat first, and then we'll go to the gendarmerie afterwards—necessary to warn them, one doesn't know what it is."

Legludic didn't say anything. I looked at him sideways; he had a very anxious face, and I saw what he was thinking.

In the end he gets up and he says to me, stubbornly: "I'm going there myself."

I look at him and I reply: "I can see you coming, Pierre . . . you have your idea . . ."

"Perhaps," he replies.

"It's not good, what you want to do. And then, it isn't prudent."

"Let it go," he says to me. "It's as if I've been drawn down there since I left. I take every step as if I had lead boots. Necessary that I go, you see. It's stronger than me. You're a brother; no one will know."

With that, he gets carried away; he starts rambling, with his eyes rolling. I'd never seen him like that. The poor devil had been living like a savage for a long time; that creature had bewildered us. After all, it wasn't my concern, it wasn't in the service. The woman laughed in our faces and didn't have the air of defending her virtue, on the contrary . . . in sum, what can I tell you, Monsieur le Commissaire Central? Perhaps I was wrong not to forbid Legludic flatly from budging from the hut. If I had known! I shouted after him but he hardly responded, and he started running. I wasn't anxious; he had his revolver. I thought that he'd come back after his caprice with that woman, who was perhaps no great thing, making fun of us.

I only became afraid when the tide turned. I called, I searched all night. Nothing. It was pitch dark. And then, this morning, there was the body of my poor Legludic lying on the sand, and no trace of the accursed creature. What did she do to him? Did she pull him under the water? They say in the neighborhood that a madwoman escaped the day before yesterday from a house in Tréguier, a young woman who'd had amorous troubles, and no one knows where she is. But if it was her we'd have the body, or one of the garments she took off, some clue . . .

No, no, Monsieur le Commissaire Central, no one will take the idea away from me that that naked being who laughed came from a country that isn't natural . . .

# THE FLOWER OF YOUTH

## by Maurice Magre

### I

THERE was once in the land of Guirec a very beautiful and very cruel princess named Raphaële. She lived in a château overlooking the sea. In the evening she liked to walk along the shore accompanied by a single hunchbacked servant who was frightful to behold. She loosened her long hair in order that it could be moistened by the perfumed wind coming from the islands. Sometimes, she played the harp on the terrace, and she took pleasure in seeing the moonlight wandering over her robe and her hands.

In the city there was a naïve and dreamy student named Joël. He was very poor, wore a torn doublet, and lived in modest lodgings in company with a dove, a dog and an old woman, who cherished him equally. The Dove, named Douce, sang love songs to him in the morning; the dog, named Ombre, went with him on his walks and caressed him with amity. The old woman, whose name was Silence, prepared his nourishment every day and taught him that in order to direct himself in life he must be sincere, courageous and good. But one evening, on the strand, Joël encountered Princess Raphaële, and he fell in love with her with all his heart.

His book no longer had any charm for him; he neglected the room in which he was accustomed to dream to the songs of the friendly dove; he consumed his days writing long elegies on the roads florid with broom and reciting them to the clouds and the sea.

In vain old Silence, who saw him growing thin and pale, enquired anxiously as to the cause of his melancholy. He remained taciturn and, at nightfall, he returned to the place on the strand where Princess Raphaële had previously appeared to him.

One evening, he was sitting, as was his custom, amid the seashells and the pebbles.

The sun had just disappeared; red flames were shining in the windows of the château that was visible on the high cliff. The tamarinds of the shore were rustling softly; a pale light trailed over the waves, and a thousand tiny benevolent faces could be seen smiling in the foam.

Joël's heart began to beat faster, for the simplicity of his soul was such that he sensed the events of his life before they happened.

In the distance, on the sand, the robe of Princess Raphaële made a sky-blue patch. She advanced, letting her hair float; her hunchbacked servant was following her.

When she was close to Joël, the latter fell to his knees and cried: "Madame, I love you more than the sea, more than the freshness of the morning and more than the verses I write in your honor. Since I have seen you, thoughts have been born in me as innumerable as the stars in the sky, and each of those thoughts speaks to me of you. Would you like to love me as I love you and to be my companion in life?"

Princess Raphaële started to laugh and looked the student up and down. But as the naivety of his eyes pleased her she said: "I forgive you, because your words are those of a child. Perhaps you do not know that I am Princess Raphaële and that I have in my service three astrologers who examine the planets in order to read my destiny therein. I know that my beauty troubles the hearts of men to the point of causing their death and I have conceived a vast ambition in consequence. I shall only love the King of France, the Devil, or the man who brings me the flower of youth."

Having said that, she drew away, and her servant gave Joël such an ugly grimace that two seabirds in the process of making love amid the algae fled in a clatter of wings.


## II


Joël remained all alone on the shore. The stars were shining in the sky; their soft light illuminated tiny gleams in the blond sand. He sat down facing the waves, feeling a great pain. He saw mist trailing over the horizon, and counted the ships passing by.

Then, in the silence of the night, he wept. And when he had wept a great deal, he placed his head on a stone and went to sleep.

Then the waves parted and a little siren appeared in the midst of the foam. Her eyes were as green as the sea when the moon is reflected in it; his skin had the whiteness of the sand; her face had the charm of candor.

She had seen the student Joël weeping and had felt pity for him. Among the sirens, as among women, pity is the sister of amour. The little siren Genofa gazed at the student Joël asleep, his eyes red and his hands joined, and she fell in love with the student Joël.

When she had watched him for some time, she took a little flower from her hair, which was pinned there, and placed it over the student's heart; then she started singing to wake him up. Her voice was musical and her words resonated softly along the cliffs.

And the powerful spirits that live in the rocks said to one another: "That's the little siren Genofa, who loves the student Joël; what will come of it?"

Joël rubbed his eyes, thinking that he was dreaming, and the little siren said to him: "You're weeping, student Joël, you must be chagrined. Look, I am beautiful, I am smiling at you, I love you. I am the sister of the sirens of the sea. Navigators sitting at the foot of their mast in the evening throw themselves into the water when they have heard us. It was to flee our enchantments that Ulysses, the wily mariner, poured wax into the ears of his companions. We are immortal; we live in damp and profound grottoes, and the delights we make known to men are infinite. Come with me to our submarine palaces. You will contemplate unknown beauties and share my eternity."

But the student Joël, putting the flower that Genofa had given him into his doublet, replied: "Certainly, O siren, your songs are agreeable and sweet to hear, but I don't desire so many marvels. My mortal eyes would be wounded by your eternal clarities. I'm human, and I prefer the temporary joy that, among humans, is accompanied by the fear of misfortune, to your cold and all too sure sensualities, which would last forever . . ."

At those words the little siren hid her face in a cluster of wrack and disappeared, allowing little white and very pure pearls to fall behind her, which were her tears.


### III


The little siren Genofa cleaved through the blue waves of the sea. Several of her companions called to her in vain; a starfish spread its futile light for her. In vain, three marine monsters smiled at her graciously. She descended ever more deeply into a region where marine flora no longer grew. She finally stopped; she had reached the entrance to the sacred grottoes where the queen of the sirens lived.

She penetrated beneath an immense vault of rocks; a sad light reigned there and sometimes caused innumerable stalactites to sparkle. There dwelt the spirits of navigators whom the sirens had charmed and caused to perish, and had rejected after having enjoyed their dead bodies. A vast groan dragged on incessantly beneath that vault; supplicant hands were raised toward the cold stone walls. A host of shades surrounded Genofa on all sides, but she had no fear of them because she knew that those forms were vain and fugitive.

There were men of every sort there.

There were mariners made illustrious by their voyages; they had seen all the lands bathed by the foamy sea; they had been returning to port on ships abundantly charged with weapons and wealth; they had already been able to see the familiar towers of their city sketched in the mist and their hearts were joyful. But they had dreamed near the sculpted prow as dusk fell. Out there, in their home, a big fire had been lit as a sign of joy; their wife was preparing the most precious wine and the most beautiful cups; their bed was ready; their servants were at the door. And for the beauty of a song, they had thrown themselves into the waves.

There were also humble fishermen. They let themselves drift into great reveries when the nights were clear; they saw luminous fish in their nets; all the protective stars were floating above their masts; every wave was a woman and, quietly, they went toward those mirages.

There were also poets that the sirens had seduced on the shore; there were men who were assumed to have lost their reason by their fellows; there were several kings, and even a mountain shepherd with his gourd and his crook, who was thinking about his goats wandering through the ferns.

They were all dreamers, and they were there because they had dreamed of the ideal on earth, and were suffering bitterly . . .

Genofa slid through the midst of all those phantoms, toward a more distant dwelling. The waves were resplendent; she had reached a blue pearl grotto that was filled by a divine music. The queen of the sirens was there, admirable for her wisdom, her power and her beauty.

Genofa said to her: "O venerated queen, welcome with benevolence the humblest of your daughters, I love a mortal, with an amour so great that it makes me hate the splendor of the seas. My heart refuses to bring him to our grottoes with the aid of our enchantments. He will only love a daughter of women of temporary beauty, but whose design would be similar to his own. Permit me, therefore, O queen, to become a woman subject to death and let me go to seek, in the light of the sun, a rapid happiness during counted days . . ."

"Imprudent and feeble child," replied the queen, "the equitable laws that regulate us do not permit me to refuse what you request, but know that, once you quit the empire of the seas, you can never again return among your sisters. Know that if you go to the world of humans you will be submissive, like them, to disease and old age, and your beautiful form will subsequently become white bones and dust."

"I am determined to make those sacrifices, wise queen," said Genofa. "Old age will be sweet to me beside my beloved. I shall bless death, if it comes to strike me one evening when we are holding hands and my eyes are contemplating the sunset."

The queen made a sign to Genofa to follow her, and took her outside the grotto with her, while the plaint of the dead deprived of light resounded, lamentable and infinite.

# IV

The student Joël had returned to his house, his heart moved by dolor. He sat down sadly beside the fire.

Douce, the dove, alighted on his shoulder and caressed his cheek with her white plumage. Ombre, the dog, lay down at his feet and licked his hands. Old Silence put a bowl of steaming soup in front of him. But he did not want to eat and said: "Do you, Silence, whose years have rendered you knowledgeable, know the flower of youth? Do you know its color, its virtue and where it can be found?"

"Certainly," the old woman replied. "It has been mentioned to me as the most precious product of nature. If I can believe what my ears have heard, its virtue is more powerful than that of all the wines matured by the sun during fecund autumns. Its gleam is as gray and dull as the evening mist, but its perfume gives those who respire it eternal youth and eternal beauty. I cannot tell you in what place on the vast earth it flowers, but it surely flowers somewhere; otherwise, its story would not occupy the evenings of human beings, for everything has a reason for being.

Instead of sleeping, Joël nourished a great project in his mind, and when the first cock sang he took his cloak and his staff and went downstairs silently.

He saw dawn break; a soft light bathed the fields and the woods, and then a vapor that trailed over the roofs and the bushes dissipated; the white road extended toward the horizon. He thought that his dove might die of solitude, that his dog might howl desperately at the sky, that the old woman would shed bitter tears in the ashes.

He closed the door firmly and drew away with long strides without looking back.

At the same time, the little siren Genofa emerged, timid and beautiful, from the blue waters. She was a woman, she was treading the fine sand joyfully, and she was going to see the man she loved.

Happy, with her moist hands, she saluted the sun . . .

# V

Joël marched along the road, and his memories rose up and fell with the dust. On the evening of the third day he met a soldier at a crossroads who was coming back from the war. He had a large feather in his cap and a long sword with a shiny hilt by his side. His stride had a proud and pleasing elegance.

"Where are you going, friend?" said the soldier to Joël. "Your clothes are covered in dust, but you seem likeable and well-informed. Night is falling, let's travel together."

"Tell me who you are and where you're going," the student replied, "in order that I know whether my route will be yours."

"My name is Glorifer and I follow the profession of arms. I've served under the King of France and I've lost more blood than I've acquired wealth. But only glory impels me; poverty is agreeable to the man who has the treasure of courage. Now I've been dismissed because there are no more wars; humankind will deteriorate from day to day. I've forgotten the place where I was born, and I'm traveling in quest of adventures."

"Come with me, then," exclaimed Joël. "I'm searching the world for the flower of youth for Princess Raphaële. When I've found it I shall marry that princess; I shall have a great kingdom and I'll appoint you as general-in-chief of my armies."

Glorifer was ambitious and that promise made him smile. He was even happier to find a companion for his route and a goal for his life. He therefore followed the student Joël.

Night had entirely fallen and they perceived the horizon of the sea. They went along a deserted strand and reached a beach in the depths of a bay. They lay down on the sand and shared a generous wine and black bread, which the soldier's gourd and knapsack contained. The Glorifer went to sleep.

He dreamed that he was in command of armies without number, that he stimulated the anger of all peoples and took rapid possession by force of arms of the empire of the earth.

The student Joël listened for a long time to the plaint of the waves; then he saw birds on a rock that were mingling their song with that of the waves. Afterwards, a crow with damp plumage arrived from the direction of the sea. It spoke in its own language to the other birds, and this is what Joël heard:

"Birds, welcome me into your flock; I am your exiled sister. My body reposes out there beneath foreign soil and I can only contemplate by night these shores dear to my heart. Oh, sing, birds; you are not dead, far from Brittany."

Then Joël wept, sensing the sadness of quitting his homeland.

## VI

The timid dawn appeared over the world and the travelers set off on the march. They arrived at the entrance to an oak wood and saw a milk-white ewe lying on the moss. Joël went to her and stroked her, because he found her beautiful. Then, as a stream was flowing not far away, he collected water in the hollow of his hand and gave it to the ewe to drink. Scarcely had she drunk than her fleece fell away, her animal body became a human body and Joël had a pale and svelte fay before him.

Glorifer, whose soul was romantic and sensible to beauty, was moved.

The fay floated momentarily above the grass and said to Joël: "You have come, traveler, to the entrance to the ancient forest of Broceliande. My name is Viviane and you have freed me from a baneful enchantment that retained me captive in the fleece of a ewe. My story is sad and marvelous. Perhaps you have heard how I was once loved by the illustrious Merlin, and how I enchained him beside me thanks to the science he had revealed to me. We were enlaced beneath a rose-bush for eternity. Alas, my amour ceased to be sufficient for him and my caresses importuned him. He succeeded in breaking the charm that retained him and he changed me into a bleating animal. I have been wandering in the woods ever since, biting in vain the bark of oaks and weeping amorous kisses. I had to remain thus until a man with a pure and loving heart offered me water in his hands. All those I have seen have thrown stones at me or tried to take me to their sheep-folds. You have come, stranger, and your kindness has rendered me beauty. But tell me what your homeland is and the goal of your journey."

"I love Princess Raphaële," replied the student, "and I'm searching for the flower of youth for her. Can you tell me who possesses it?"

"I believe that at this moment it is still in the hands of the illustrious Merlin, who has respired it and is handsome and immortal. Plunge into these forests; perhaps you will find him there, prey to meditation. You'll recognize him by the nobility of his face. Speak to him without fear, imploring him. He is good, even though he has made me suffer; he will listen to you and grant your plea."

Joël thanked the fay, and was getting ready to leave, joyfully, followed by Glorifer, when Viviane called him back and said to him, blushing: "If you see him out there, tell him that I have recovered my form as a woman, and if you have found charm in my eyes, tell him that too. You can add that I still love him, that I am waiting for him, my hair undone, under the willows, and that I am singing his praises to the birds of the forest and the broom of the heath."

Joël and Glorifer wandered for several days through the clearings and the thickets. They nourished themselves on wild fruits and slept in the hollows of oaks.

They arrived in a place where the bushes were so dense that Glorifer was obliged to separate them with his sword. They saw a spring flowing in a clearing; they ran to it. Near the water, a man was dreaming, with his head in his hands. He was tall and venerable, and the travelers recognized Merlin.

Joël prostrated himself at his feet and told him about his journey and how he had come to seek the flower of youth. Then Merlin, after having heard him, raised his arms toward the vault of verdure, agitated his beard and exclaimed:

"Insensate traveler! You are preparing the worst of your woes. Look at me: I am suffering and nothing can console me. Once my youthful desire embraced the universe; I led, joyfully, the career of life and the solitude of my mind stimulated my ardor. But I fell in love! I respired the flower of youth in order that time would not erode the beautiful white marble of our amour. I have known the monotonous joy of endless dreams. The amour that lasts forever is the greatest of tortures, Child! Old age and death are the great friends that console our soul."

"O Merlin, under these profound forests, in the shade of these bushes, among the myrtle and the broom, you have loved in the manner of humans. I also love; understand my heart and grant my plea."

"I will not go against your destiny," replied Merlin. "Can one ever have only oneself to blame for one's misfortune? The flower of youth was stolen from me once by Moch, the spirit of the sands. He took it to Dehut, the daughter of Gradlon, King of Ys, who offered her kisses at that price. But the anger of the heavens prevented that union. The waves of the sea engulfed the city of Ys one evening, for Dehut's impurity wearied God. Go to the nearest shore; when you see a rock that has the form of a sleeping crow, stop. There dwells Moch, the spirit of the sands. Perhaps he has kept the flower of youth. I can do nothing more for you; I no longer know anything. I have lost my power, amour has corroded my mind like a wound."

Having said that, Merlin fell back into his meditations; but Joël, as he was about to draw away, remembered Viviane and said to him: "O Merlin, listen to me again. I have liberated a fay hidden in the body of a white ewe. She is marvelously beautiful. She told me that her name is Viviane, and that she loves you."

Scarcely had he spoke those words than Merlin's face expressed a horrible terror. He got up and cried: "Viviane is free! Accursed be the beauty that has caused my eyes to dream, accursed be the flesh that has given pleasure to my flesh! If I encounter her under these trees she will enchain me in the prison of her arms. To the sterile sensuality of amour I prefer the unconsciousness of stone!"

Merlin cut an oak branch and drew a circle around himself. In the place where he had been standing, his eyes sparkling with light, there was no longer anything but a great melancholy rock. For all eternity, Merlin had returned to the bosom of his august mother, the earth, of whom he was the most illustrious son. He still reposes out there, invisible for our mortal eyes, amid the rosemary, under the gray fogs of Armorica . . .

Joël and Glorifer saluted the silent rock with a long adieu, and then they drew away through the forest.

# VII

After having reached the sea, they went along the shore for some time, and they stopped in the house of an old mariner.

There they made the acquaintance of Tinah, the gatherer of seaweed, whose eyes were as blue as the horizon. She was still a child; she lived alone on the shore, awaiting the return of her father, who had departed three years before. Every evening, when the tide went out, she shed tears, because she thought that he was dead. Every evening, however, she lit the fire and set another place for him at the wooden table.

She linked herself in amity with the travelers; she told them the story of her petty life, her chagrins, and her great hope of seeing her father's sail appear on the sea.

Joël and Glorifer stayed there for several days. While Joël dreamed about Princess Rafaële, Glorifer accompanied Tinah over the shingle and told her the story of his adventures. Once, he had cut a bridge with a single stroke of his sword; another time, like Samson, he had broken the columns of a temple in order to crush his enemies.

Tinah pretended to take a great interest in such exploits, but she often questioned the soldier about the cares of his friend. Joël intimidated her, even though he was almost the same age as her. She could not speak to him without blushing, and fearfully.

One evening, while he was sitting down and gazing at the stars, she took his hand gently in hers and said: "It's not necessary to be chagrined, student Joël . . ." But then she turned away and hid her face.

That evening, the travelers decided that it was time to leave, and that they would set forth again at dawn.

When dawn came, Tinah walked with them along the shore. She told them that a rock similar to a sleeping crow was situated a short distance away. Moch, the spirit of the sands, lived in a deep cavern; he was a cruel and strong old man who challenged fishermen to wrestle and put them to death when he had defeated them.

"Have courage," she said, when she quit them. "I shall pray for you, and you will be illustrious heroes. I shall wait for my father on the beach, and the sound of the waves will remind me of you."

In the distance, she extended her small white hand toward them. Glorifer waved his long arms and his big feather so many times that the birds passing by were frightened. And when, on turning round, they could no longer see Tinah's dress, he pulled his hat down over his eyes in order that the student Joël would not be witness to his weakness.

They found the spirit of the sands asleep in his cave. Joël approached him and woke him up by tugging gently on his beard. Then Moch got up, prey to a great anger, and challenged them to fight.

Having put down his sword, Glorifer exhorted Joël to stay by the cave entrance, and he took the old man in his arms.

Their struggle lasted for several hours; after that time, Glorifer had the spirit of the sands under his knee;

the latter asked for mercy and promised to realize the travelers' desire. Glorifer help his adversary to his feet and wiped away the dust covering his body.

When Joël had explained why he had come, Moch replied, weeping:

"I've been defeated in wrestling, and I certainly experience a great dolor because of it, but that dolor is nothing compared to the one that your words reanimate in my soul. I loved the daughter of the King of Ys, but my lips never touched hers. She was the most beautiful of all the women whose eyes have contemplated the sea. She surrendered her flesh to those who desired it but my amour was all the more ardent for that. Her sins are illustrious throughout these shores.

"I stole the flower of youth for her, but the waves invaded the city of Ys just as I arrived there to offer it to her. I saw her, voluptuous until death when the waves carried her away. Then I threw the flower of youth away, and I fled weeping.

"It's in thinking of her that I immolate my victims. I see her eyes in the stars, her hair in the wrack, and her heart in the sun. You're fortunate, stranger, to love a woman; amour alone is beautiful!"

His eyes were full of tears and he let long moans escape. However, he added: "I remember that a traveler captive in my cave mentioned the flower of youth to me. He told me that the waves had cast it up on a shore where an astrologer named Asmodius had found it. That astrologer departed for the palace of King Louis XI, who, fearing death more than life, has promised immense treasures and great honors in exchange for the flower of youth."

196

Joël and Glorifer had heard enough; they left Moch, the spirit of the sands, to continue his lamentations. They emerged from his abode, glad to see the light of the sky again.

The sun had just disappeared over the horizon; a blue mist floated over the water; it was the time when the powerful spirits who inhabit the rocks exchange solemn words between themselves like the sounds of the wind. The first star made its light tremble; the travelers gazed at the sea.

Under the transparent waves they perceived great ruined towers and the phantoms of palaces, the shade of a city. It was Ys, the melancholy and misfortunate city asleep on the ocean bed.

And slowly, in the religious silence of the falling night, one by one, bells rang with a distant, mysterious and beautiful sound. Their voice resonated over the cliffs and the distant islands, like human sobbing.

Joël and Glorifer saw errant forms trailing over the sea, twisting their arms; they advanced toward them and could already hear their sighs; but they fled, frightened, in the direction of the land.

## VIII

They marched for several days toward the capital of the kingdom of France. On the way, they encountered a dwarf who was fighting with an eagle. The dwarf was little and old; the eagle was powerful, and was holding the dwarf's hood in its beak, trying to lift him into the air.

Moved by pity, Joël ran forward and struck the eagle with his staff. Glorifer thrust at it with his sword and the eagle fled, staining the treetops with its blood.

The dwarf that Joël had saved was jovial and benevolent; he was a forest dwarf. He made several pirouettes and picked several daisies as a sign of joy, for dwarfs have simple and puerile souls. Then he said to Joël:

"I live in the profound earth and I am a friend of the oaks. My name is Mus. Take this whistle; if you're ever in danger, call me, and you'll see that dwarfs are not ingrates."

And he went away, singing.

The next day, Joël and Glorifer saw towers appear in the distance in large numbers, and they understood that they had reached Paris, the city of King Louis XI. They stopped in a meadow to get a little rest and brighten up their garments.

Glorifer went to sleep, and while he slept, Joël perceived some distance away an orchard full of blonde apples. The fruits tempted him and he ran to the trees to pick some. The apples had an admirable taste and he ate several. He was about to go and wake his friend, but six of the king's archers who were passing by threw themselves upon him; he had been eating apples from the royal orchard.

Joël tried to struggle, but the archers were very strong; he cried out, but Glorifer's slumber was very profound. Joël therefore entered Paris as a captive, as a thief.

When they arrived in the city the leader of the archers asked him whether he knew a minister, a bishop or a noble of the court, in which case he could be released.

Joël replied that he was a student and had come from Brittany. Then he was taken to prison and was assured that he would be hanged in three days' time.

Joël believed in his lucky star. On the first evening he searched the sky through the bars of his dungeon for its friendly light. There was one that was brighter and softer than all the rest; he thought that it was his, and went to sleep dreaming about Raphaële.

On the second evening he remembered the whistle given to him by the dwarf Mus. He put his head to the narrow skylight from which he could still see a corner of the world. The Seine curved silently at the foot of his prison; the somber city reposed in the distance. He inflated his cheeks and blew with all his might. The walls did not crumble; the footsteps of a jailer resonated in the corridor. Joël threw the whistle into the water and a great anxiety entered his heart.

On the third evening, thinking that he only had a few more hours to live, he wept. He saw again the house in his homeland, the woman he loved and his companion Glorifer.

Then he heard a rattle of keys, and the jailer who was accustomed to bring him bread and water at that hour came in. He seemed to Joël to be shorter than usual; he raised his lantern and Joël recognized the jovial face of the dwarf Mus.

The latter took him by the hand and drew him through the somber corridors and stairways of the prison. Joël noticed that the sentinels they passed were all little bearded men who made comical grimaces of amity at Mus. They arrived in the courtyard and there Joël perceived the bodies of men bound and gagged. Instead of the archers of the guard post there were dwarfs who were playing games. The gate was wide open; Joël ran outside; he was free. Before he had recovered from his astonishment, the prison closed again; the dwarf Mus had disappeared.

The student perceived a church. He lay down under the porch and went to sleep, for he was very tired. At dawn a doorkeeper and a cruel priest woke him up brutally and drove him away. In those days, the priests readily deemed that it was only necessary to be good to the rich.

Joël moved on, and as he went he asked an artisan where Louis XI lived; it was in the king's abode that he counted on finding the flower of youth.

He was told that the King's residence was in a place called Plessis and that the people were waiting impatiently for him to die, for the sovereign feared death for himself but lavished it on his subjects. He lived in prayer, surrounded by holy images, while honest men rendered their souls at Montfaucon on his orders, while cursing God.

Joël set forth to walk to Plessis and arrived there after several days as the sun was setting. He wandered in the city for some time and perceived that an extraordinary joy reigned there. The taverns were resounding with songs and young students like him were going through the streets arm in arm.

*King Louis XI must have respired the flower of youth,* Joël thought, *and wants the people to rejoice.*

He arrived at the royal dwelling. It was a crenellated fortress surrounded by a broad moat. The drawbridge was lowered; nearby, soldiers were drinking and playing cards; many were drunk. Night had fallen.

Joël went into the courtyard without being noticed, climbed a staircase, and went through a few halls, taking advantage of the general disorder. There were people running hither and yon, others banqueting at tables; others were groaning, but their laments had something discordant and false about them.

Several times, Joël heard cries of "Vive le dauphin!" and he thought that the King was dead.[1] The cries of a weeping woman resounded; that was perhaps the most sincere grief.

Then there were the sounds of instruments; musicians and shepherds were playing lutes and flutes. The king had sent for them in order that their music would keep him awake for as long as possible as the great sleep approached. Now they were creating joyful sounds for the ears of the living; then they would return home to recount the death of the king and the large salary they had received.

Joël perceived a lamp at the end of a corridor. The lamp in question was flickering in a narrow room with thick walls. There was a door studded with iron nails and bolts. The window was barred; a star was smiling there. And at the back, on the bed, gray, ugly, humble, solitary and shrunken, the king was lying.

He had done everything he could, the poor king. She had come, the one he feared more than the Duc de

---

1 Louis XI died on 30 August 1483.

Bretagne or Charles le Téméraire. The doors were firmly shut; the halberdiers were watching on the towers; how had she got in? What somber wrath animated her, in order that in squeezing the temples, she had spread so much horror over that visage?

Joël fled, full of dolor and terror.

## IX

He went back to Paris with the hope of finding his companion Glorifer and learning what had become of the flower of youth. He wandered for some time from one crossroads to another and one hostelry to another. He could see that the change of sovereign had not transformed the State. Beggars continued to be hungry, bourgeois to die in abundance in their houses, and priests to honor God at the expense of men. And he was greatly astonished by that.

One evening, as he was going along a dark street, he saw an old man sitting on a stone, who was weeping. As his soul was charitable, he went to him and asked him the cause of his tears.

The old man had child-like eyes and was making the gestures of a madman. He cried: "I'm a dreamer, Monsieur. You see before you the most unfortunate of astrologers. I have spent my days reading the secrets of the world in the stars. I can say that I have lived in the sky. At the end of my life I loved a woman; she was beautiful and loved me for the beauty of my dreams. She understood that the ideal must be detached from all material preoccupation, and I always found in her home a table ornamented by light, sought-after dishes and virtuous bottles. I loved her, Monsieur, and she betrayed me for a soldier."

Joël consoled him with soft words and asked him how it had happened.

"My marriage," the astrologer replied, "was already arranged with Simone, the beautiful proprietress of the Cheval Rouge. A couple so united had never been seen. I dreamed and she worked. But one day, when we were in the large room of the hostelry, a soldier came in. He seemed to be poor, but had the arrogance of a Maréchal. He told her to bring him all the wine in our casks, for he had a great sorrow to drown, and then he wept. Aided by one of Simone's soldiers I tried to put him outside gently; he drew his sword and threatened to kill us all. It was at that moment that Simone commenced to love him. He had the coarse beauty of men of war. We served him drinks, he put Simone on his knees and kissed her in front of me, and as I was gripped by a just indignation he threw me out violently. God knows what he has eaten and drunk since! Simone loves him and is going to marry him. The hostelry has become a subject of scandal; the soldier is perpetually drunk and invites passers-by to drink with him. The table is open to all the paupers of the street and Simone, once so orderly, opens the oldest vintages herself. I've gone there disguised as a beggar and have been treated like a king without opening my purse. Is that not shameful?"

Joël was on the track of his companion. He begged the old man urgently to take him to the hostelry of the

Cheval Rouge; he might be able to soothe his woes. The latter agreed readily, and on the way he said:

"My name is Asmodius and the greatest destiny was promised to me. I nearly became as powerful as the King of France, for I nearly saved him from death. I had found the flower of youth and I was taking it to him attached to my staff, in order that it should seem devoid of value and that no one would steal it from me; but the bird Orock, who lives in the Caucasus Mountains, passed by and stole it from me. What has become of it now?"

When they reached the hostelry Joël's heart was full of joy. The old man's dolor became indignation; a flame of wrath was shining in his eyes. The joyous sound of songs and clinking glasses was audible; the scene of the feast was visible through the windows.

There was a large number of guests of all sorts: bourgeois whom the abundance of wine caused to forget their dignity; drunkards made illustrious by their prowess; a gallant abbé who was talking amorously to a young woman with a naïve gaze; avid paupers taking advantage with all their might of such a windfall; and two young lovers who were affecting to drink from the same glass. In the middle, under her admirably white coiffure, the beautiful Simone was radiant. And Joël perceived beside her the worthy Glorifer, in person, drinking, his face serene, and displaying in his attitudes the grandeur of his martial and sentimental soul.

The beautiful Simone was standing up, she had a cup full of golden wine and was about to drink to the health of her lover, and all the guests were attentive.

But the astrologer could stand it no longer. He opened the door abruptly, irrupted into the room and launched himself toward the woman who had betrayed him. He cried:

"Oh, thrice ingrate who has snatched me from sacred dreams for fleeting lusts. The planets have spoken to me this evening in a puerile language that does my old age good. In the woods or before the sea I understood them and I was happy. Render me all the beautiful things that you have made me hate. You have destroyed my high prestige and have rendered me an object of derision. I demand your body and your house in exchange for my lost dreams . . ."

A great stupor was painted on all faces; one of the paupers hid a ham under his doublet; the two young lovers, holding one another tightly, gazed at human misfortunes with indifference. All eyes turned to Glorifer.

But at that moment the table collapsed, the candles went out and the guests were knocked down. Glorifer had perceived Joël on the threshold of the house, had bounded forward and fallen into his arms.

An indescribable tumult reigned in the darkness; there were cries, and the sound of shattering glass and breaking porcelain; the lovers hugged one another more ardently; the bourgeois invoked reason; the abbé groped for his neighbor; the paupers set forth in pursuit of the food; the beautiful Simone was heard sobbing.

Glorifer closed the door behind him and drew his companion through the streets in haste.

# X

Joël and Glorifer had resumed their journey and were wandering the world again in search of the redoubtable bird Orock. They slept in fields or under trees; sometimes they received kind hospitality in houses, and Glorifer caused astonishment by the facility he had in eating and drinking.

They had left the land of France a long time ago when they arrived in a city where the men drank beer of an admirable color and almost all the women were pretty.

It was Sunday; the taverns were full of joyful drunkards; the smoke of pipes rose so thickly that it obscured the light of the sun. A mild peace seemed to possess all hearts. Young women were strolling on the promenades wearing new bonnets and their finest dresses. Audacious clerks were following close behind them, and more than one kiss was audible in the solitary pathways.

Joël saw peasants dancing in the shade of linden trees and he thought about his homeland. How sweet it must be to love with simplicity like that, on Sundays, to the sound of violins, and then resume quotidian labors!

A man laden with years had just passed by. Everyone saluted him respectfully, even the most beautiful women, who usually had no thought of anything but amour.

Joël asked who the old man was and was told that he was the illustrious Dr. Faust, renowned for his wisdom and his science. Joël resolved to go and interrogate him about the flower of youth, in the hope of obtaining some precious indication. When dusk fell he went to his dwelling, while Glorifer waited for him in front of a large tankard of beer.

Conducted by the disciple Wagner, Joël went into a room with a high ceiling. A lamp made its yellow light tremble over the dusty leather of books, and sad rows of bottles, jars and instruments. A death's-head posed on the table seemed ready to cry to the visitor: *I'm the master of the house. What do you want?*

At the back, in his armchair, Dr. Faust was dreaming.

Then Joël told him about his travels and why he was undertaking them.

Faust said to him: "You envy my science, child! I am the most ignorant of men, and there is no rude manual laborer on earth who does not have more science than me. You've come to interrogate me! But I am the one who should have come to you like a pilgrim with a hazel-wood staff and a cloak the color of the road; you could have taught me the sweetness of loving a woman and thinking about her in the evening, while going to sleep in a meadow. Alas, during all the nights of my youth, I searched in the depths of books for the light of verity. It filtered over my table with the moon's rays, as it does today, but I did not understand it. Now I've attained the arid kingdom of wisdom and I remember with bitter regret the beautiful domain of the foolish. Happy are the fools! They march like blind men, and yet they do not fall into wells, like sages. What gay companions fantasy and caprice are! Sleep under the dust, excessively veridical books! Cease laughing, O death's-head! Give me a fool's bauble and bells, and also your heart, young student!"

Faust began to groan, and then fell into a somber reverie, while Joël went away silently.

# XI

The two travelers wandered in lands without number. They traversed great rivers bordered with palm trees, climbed mountains devoid of flowers, contemplated luminous cities. They saw people made ugly and short by a rigorous climate, and others to whom a propitious sunlight gave harmonious forms. There were some who worshiped the moon, others who worshiped fire and the wind, others who worshiped animals, others who worshiped an invisible and abstract God, and others who did not worship any God at all. Among all of them they found the same passions and the same dreams; all were obliged to seek their nourishment on the land and all feared death.

Three years had passed since Joël and Glorifer had left the city of the savant Faust when they reached the sea of a thousand waves. On the somber shores they found an honest and peaceful seafaring people. They were welcomed joyfully, and then elected kings by those men expert in manipulating oars. Their reign lasted nine days, and at the end of that time they chartered a ship and departed over the waves, guided by skillful pilots.

A violent tempest soon rose; the wind carried away the sails. The stars were the color of blood. The vessel broke up on reefs and was engulfed, but Joël and Glorofer clung on to a mast and confided themselves to the impetuous winds. In the rain and the darkness, they were cast on to an isolated rock, similar to a God.

There they found a man sitting alone in the midst of the foam. A similar misfortune united them and they embraced, full of love for one another.

"Doubtless you've been saved, like us, from some terrible shipwreck?" said the student.

"I'm accustomed to these adventures," the stranger replied. "I love the proximity of death. I've escaped the Old Man of the Sea, the Trembling Island, and the giants that only have one eye in the forehead. I have riches that twenty ships couldn't carry; in India I've found the largest diamonds that exist; I would even possess the flower of youth, which I stole from the bird Orock seven years ago, if I hadn't let it fall into the sea. I'm illustrious in Bagdad for my voyages, and my name is Sinbad."

Having said that, he stood up, showed his companions a tremulous light that had just appeared in the distance and had to be the beacon of a ship, and, having exhorted Joël and Glorifer to follow him, he launched himself into the waves.

They saw him struggling momentarily against the tempest, but the darkness was intense; they could no longer hear anything but a long cry that was lost in the roar of the wind and the plaint of the sea.

Joël perceived then that Glorifer's head, which had collided with the rocks, was bleeding abundantly. And the latter, sensing that his hour had come, said:

"Student Joël, you'll appoint another man than me as general of your armies. I shall not have known glory among men, but I believe that God will give me a large troop to command in Paradise. If you pass the hostelry of the Cheval Rouge again, tell the beautiful Simone that I was thinking about her as I died. And you, my dear companion, who love me, remain joyful in dolor, good in prosperity and always march through life heroically . . ."

Glorifer opened his arms, made a comical and resigned grimace, looked at the sky and died.

The sea had calmed down and the student Joël's tears fell one by one into the quiet waves. The darkness dissipated, and when morning appeared, passing sailors came to take the student Joël off the rock where his friend was sleeping forever.

He stayed at the stern of the ship, overwhelmed by grief, his eyes staring at the fatal rock.

In the distance he could see the brave Glorifer extended, motionless and stiff, as if on parade, amid the blue wrack and the gentle foam. And he, therefore, was going to resume the course of the endless journey alone. For the first time, his heart failed.

Dawn illuminated the world and the song of the pilot rang out. Every tear shed was a little benevolent spirit that was to follow him over the luminous sea and then over the obscure land, for the tears of friendship are the only ones that never perish . . .

## XII

Joël had been set down by the mariners on an unknown shore. Inhospitable men lived there, who did not welcome travelers in their houses, and Joël marched in the direction opposed to the sea. The land seemed disinherited and misfortunate; an eternal mist enveloped it; there were arid valleys and mountains planted with fir trees. The stars that floated over those landscapes were yellow or red, and their light sowed terror and desolation. There were pools of glaucous water and the divinities of those marshes were ugly and groaning.

Leaning on his staff, Joël advanced through that country. His heart was so sad that he was inaccessible to fear; he understood that he was about to reach the limits of the world and only his curiosity guided him. He climbed terrible summits where the rocks and the clouds were confounded; he went past lakes as profound as the earth, where green beings lived, which gazed at him with a single enormous eye and were not endowed with movement. He no longer saw birds overhead. He descended precipitate slopes and traversed mysterious plains. Several times, he thought he saw white phantoms fleeing as he approached, but he thought that they were mirages of his mind caused by fatigue and excitement.

It had been several days since Joël had seen any sign of human life, and he felt that he was about to die of it. Darkness covered the earth, his feet were bleeding, his brain was empty and bleak—and then he perceived a light.

He marched rapidly in that direction and reached a little house. Around it there were trees and a garden with flowers. The door stood ajar; he opened it and went in. He found a bed, a table, a stool, a loaf of bread and a pitcher of water. In the ashes of the fire a black dog was whining. Joël sat down and shared the bread and water with the dog; then the latter licked his hands and died.

Joël was ready to go to bed, but he went outside to see whether the master of the house was in the garden. He took a few steps along a path; roses were shedding their petals there and he took great pleasure in respiring them. He continued walking and saw a ditch as narrow and deep as a grave. A little further on, he stumbled over a recumbent man, and a terrible fear gripped him. He felt him with his trembling hands; he was dead. He must have been extraordinarily old.

Then, although he was exhausted by fatigue and chilled by terror, he dragged the dead man to the grave and covered him with pious earth. Then he went back into the house and went to sleep.

After he had slept for a few hours, a strange light filled the room and woke him up, Joël saw the old man that he had buried standing beside him. He was handsome and seemed just; his rags were radiant. He spoke.

"This evening, you have laid beneath the clement earth the body of the most indefatigable pilgrim that the sun has ever illuminated. My name is Isaac Laquedem. I am the man who said to Jesus Christ: 'Go on your way, my dwelling is not yours.' He avenged himself on me cruelly although he professed to forgive sins. Since then I have traveled the vast world, I have listened to people cursing me in various tongues and I became more powerful than God, my master, because I have seen men suffering.

"Then I set down my staff and I cried: 'My task is concluded, Lord! I want to see three last sunsets, in a flowery garden, near a house at the limits of the world, only having the amity of a dog, and to die thereafter.'

212

My wish has been granted. You arrived, child, as I died. You gave bread to my dog and earth to my remains. I want to recompense you and terminate your journey. You have been searching for seven years for the flower of youth without knowing that the flower in question was against your breast. It was given to you on a shore by a siren who loved you, and fatality has laughed at you."

Joël put his hand into his doublet; there was indeed a little flower there; it was gray and devoid of beauty. He remembered, then, that he had taken it unthinkingly from the hands of the siren Genofa, one evening when he had gone to sleep on the shore.

There it was, then, the flower that the mariner Sinbad had dropped into the sea, and which the waves must have tossed until Genofa had made an ornament for her hair with it.

For seven years he had been traveling the world in search of a prize that he had on his person. For seven years, instead of wandering miserably, he could have tasted the happiness of which he dreamed.

Dolor took possession of him at that thought, but the old man went on:

"I will take you back to the town where you were born, but on condition that you always remain good. Know that if you ever cause the death of a child, a maiden or a beggar—which is to say, a pure soul—on that day I will take back the life that I have given you, and on that day you will be no more than a pinch of dust carried away by the evening breeze . . ."

Joël remained motionless, prey to astonishment. The old man took him in his arms and carried him away through the air.

# XII

Joël found himself sitting on the side of a road. He must have been traveling for a night and a day, for the sun was setting. He was holding the flower of youth in his hand; he was alone. He looked around; the woods and the fields were familiar to him; a friendly perfume rose from the fields; his native earth embalmed his soul. Close by, there was a clump of trees, where he had often dreamed in his youth. The steeple rose up in the azure in the distance, like a benevolent and ironic smile.

Bewildered by joy, Joël started running along the road. He would have liked to kiss those objects, the sight of which was so sweet to him, to hug the rude soil to his breast. An infinite emotion invaded him, a happiness of which he had not believed his human nature capable.

The sea was paling on the horizon; the sun gilded the wheat; he saw doves in a field. They started to laugh and greeted him: "*Bonjour! Bonjour!*" they said "We recognize you, student Joël; you've been on a long journey! One of our companions died last year, weeping for you copiously . . ."

A little further on he saw a dog passing by and heard it murmuring in its own language: "Isn't that the student Joël who left seven years ago? Ombre, my brother, won't lick his hands and face, for I saw him die last winter . . ."

Then there was an old woman carrying a faggot of dead wood, who crossed herself on seeing him, and said:

"Phantom of student Joël, it's doubtless your punishment to wander the earth. How remorse must be making you suffer! Old Silence, who loved you so much, shed tears as numerous as the leaves of spring, and dolor caused her death . . ."

Joël stopped, his heart lacerated. All the beings that were dear to him had departed from his house, then, taken away by a pitiless destiny. Had his amour not been inconsiderate? Had he not been bound to sacrifice the dove, the dog and the old woman to it? He thought that one cannot struggle against one's passions, that at that very moment, his amour was triumphing over his misfortunes.

He held the flower of youth in his right hand and he marched, his eyes fixed, toward Princess Raphaële's château.

He saw a young woman coming toward him; she had eyes the color of the sea. It was the little siren Genofa.

For seven years she had been waiting for the student Joël. She lived in a sheepfold near the road and was desolate, every evening, when the footsteps of a traveler resounded.

This evening, her eyes were full of tears, but those tears became a smile, and the smile an ecstasy, and she ran forward, her arms extended, toward the man who was approaching.

O joy! It really was the student Joël, the student Joël who had been thinking about her, who loved her, since he was holding like a talisman, as he returned to his village, the flower that she had once given him. So they were finally going to love one another! She was mute with joy.

But why was he not saying anything? Why was he not crying out: "It's me!" and taking her in his arms?

He looked at her with astonishment, searching his memories in vain. Then, with a gesture to evoke the entire past, she said: "Would you like to return that flower to me, Monsieur Student?"

But he started to laugh, and replied: "It's the flower of youth, for which I've been searching for seven years, and which I'm taking to Princess Raphaële, Mademoiselle Shepherdess . . ."

And, saluting her with his hand, he passed on.

The sea breeze inflated his cloak and he marked his footprints in the sand of the shore joyfully. He was very close to the princess's château. He saw the first stars born over the sea; he heard a delightful music of harps and, raising his eyes, he perceived instrument-players on the high terrace. And in front of them, beneath her loose black hair and her sky blue dress, in the mirage of the nascent moon, as beautiful as the waves and dreams, Princess Raphaële was gazing at the horizon.

Joël arrived at the stone stairway. One more minute and he would be at the feet of his beloved and a little joy would redeem his long woes. He had reached the end of his journey, and an infinite happiness filled his soul. He fell to his knees and thanked God.

At that same instant, in the distance, on the edge of the white road, the little siren Genofa, her hands crossed over her chaste and patient heart, expired.

And the prediction of the Wandering Jew was accomplished.

Joël had caused a virgin to die of love, and in the place where he had been kneeling, praising the Lord, there was no longer anything but a pinch of dust, which the evening breeze blew into the sea.

Thus destiny and amour play cruelly with men . . .

# ACKNOWLEDGEMENTS

PAUL ARÈNE (1843-1896) was a Provencal writer who wrote Occitan poetry as well as producing work abundantly in French. He worked in collaboration with Alphonse Daudet on the latter's documentary *Lettres du mon Moulin* (1869). "La Calanques des sirens" first appeared in *L'Écho de Paris* 13 March 1892, and "Le Nid des sirènes" in *Le Journal* 9 March 1896. "Sirens' Creek" and "A Sirens' Nest" are both original to the present volume.

LUCIE DELARUE-MARDRUS (1874-1945) was a prolific poet, sculptor, novelist and journalist who was a regular contributor to *Le Journal* for forty years. She was married to the physician and Oriental scholar J. C. Mardrus between 1900 and 1915 but was also an intimate member of Natalie Barney's circle, along with Renée Vivien, and was awarded the first Renée Vivien prize for poetry in 1936. "La Dernière sirène" was first published in *Le Journal* 8 July 1908. "The Last Siren" first appeared as the title story of a collection of Delarue-Mardrus' works.

REMY DE GOURMONT (1858-1915) was the most important literary critic of his era, and his studies of authors involved in the Symbolist Movement, many of them collected in *Le Livre des masques* (1896) and *Le Deuxième Livre des Masques* (1898), provided an invaluable map of its extent and commentary on its ambitions. He was one of the founders of the *Mercure de France* and became its most prolific contributor, developing his distinctive short fiction in its pages. Disfigured by lupus, he became a recluse before the century ended, and his health deteriorated steadily thereafter, although he kept on writing relentlessly while he could. "La Dame pensive" and "La Sirène innocente" were both reprinted in *D'un pays lointain* (1898; tr. as *From a Faraway Land*); "The Pensive Lady" and "The Innocent Siren" both appeared in the translation of that collection in 2019.

BERNARD LAZARE was the pen-name of Lazare Bernard (1865-1903), a political journalist and short story writer who took a leading role in the Dreyfus Affair. "La Dernière sirène" appeared in his anarchist portmanteau *Les Porteurs des torches* (1897; tr. as *The Torch-Bearers*), and as "The Last Siren" in the 2019 translation of that work.

CAMILLE LEMONNIER (1844-1913) was a Belgian writer who became one of the older members of the Jeune Belgique clique affiliated to the Symbolist Movement, although most of his work consists of Naturalist accounts of peasant life. He was prosecuted three times for allegedly offending public morals but only convicted and fined once. "La Petite femme de la mer" first appeared in *La Revue illustrée* 1 July 1897 before being reprinted in the *Mercure de France* and as the title story of a collection in 1898. "The Little Woman of the Sea" is original to the present volume.

MAURICE MAGRE (1877-1941) was a prolific poet, novelist and dramatist with strong Decadent affiliations, the finest French writer of fantastic fiction in the first half of the twentieth century. "Le Fleur de jeunesse" first appeared in his collection *Histoire merveilleuse de Claire d'Amour* (1903) and "La Dernière Siren" in the November 1905 issue of *La Nouvelle Revue*. "The Flower of Youth" and "The Last Siren" both appeared in *The Marvelous Story of Claire d'Amour and Other Stories*, the first of a twelve-volume set of translations of Magre's works.

CAMILLE MAUCLAIR was the pseudonym of Séverin Faust (1872-1945), a regular at Stéphane Mallarmé's *mardis* when young, who described that clique in his *roman à clef Les Soleil des morts* (1898), and remained affiliated to Mallarmé's literary theories throughout his career, although most of his later work was non-fiction. "La Pêcheuse des hommes" first appeared in *Le Journal* 22 August 1906; "The Fisher of Men" is original to the present volume.

CATULLE MENDÈS (1841-1909) was a protégé of Théophile Gautier in the early years of his career. His unproduced drama *Roman d'une nuit* (1861) was prosecuted for obscenity, landing him in prison for a month.

He was extraordinarily adaptable and prolific, producing an enormous amount of short fiction for newspapers. His novels *Zo'har* (1886) and *Méphistophela* (1890; tr. as *Mephistophela*) were crucial contributions to the Decadent Movement. "La Tristesse des sirènes" appeared in the collection *Le Rose et le noir* (1885); "The Sorrow of the Sirens" first appeared in *Don Juan in Paradise and Other Amorous Fantasies* (2019).

PIERRE MILLE (1864-1941) was a prolific and successful journalist who had a prize for reportage named after him. Most of his books are non-fiction, but they include several collections of short stories. "Les sirènes" first appeared in *Le Journal* 10 May 1907 and "La dernière sirène" in *Le Journal* 7 June 1920. "The Sirens" and "The Last Siren" are original to the present volume.

ARNOLD MORTIER (1843-1885) was a journalist best known for drama criticism and a playwright who contributed to the librettos for two light operas by Jacques Offenbach based on works by Jules Verne, *Le Docteur Ox* (1877) and the spectacular *Le Voyage dans le lune* (1875). "L'Homme de la Mer" first appeared in *Le Figaro* on 4 November 1883. "The Man of the Sea" is original to the present collection.

HENRI DE RÉGNIER (1864-1936) formed a friendship at school with Egbert Viélé, who began signing himself Francis Viélé-Griffin when the two of them became Symbolist poets; the two founded *Entretiens politiques et littéraires* in collaboration with Paul Adam in 1890. Régnier published his own "Symbolist Manifesto" in

*Le Bosquet de Psyché* (1894) and several collections of Symbolist prose, most notably *La Canne de jaspe* (1897), which included "Aventure marine et amoureuse." "An Amorous Adventure at Sea" first appeared in *A Surfeit of Mirrors: Symbolist Tales and Uncertain Stories* (2012).

MAURICE RENARD (1875-1939) was the great pioneer and propagandist of "scientific marvel fiction," a species of *roman scientifique* distinguished from Vernian fiction but not its more adventurous speculations, although he also made significant contributions to the genres of crime fiction and supernatural fiction. "La Cantatrice" appeared in *Monsieur d'Outremort et autres histories singuliers* (1913) "The Cantatrice" first appeared in *The Doctored Man and Other Stories* (2010; the fourth volume in a five-volume series collectively entitled *The Scientific Marvel Fiction of Maurice Renard*).

RENÉE VIVIEN was the pseudonym of Pauline Tarn (1877-1909), an English-born Decadent and Symbolist poet, now best known for her membership of a Parisian lesbian clique centered on the salon of the American writer Nathalie Barney, and for her Sapphic poetry. "Le Chant des sirènes" appeared in *Du vert au violet* (1903) and "Les Sirènes ne chantent plus" (1904) in *Copeaux*, signed by Hélène de Zuylen de Nyevelt (Hélène van Zuylen, 1863-1947), Vivien's collaborator at the time, although it is almost certainly Vivien's work. "The Song of the Sirens" first appeared in *Lilith's Legacy: Prose Poems and Short Stories* (2018) and "The Sirens No Longer Sing" in *Faustina and Other Stories* (2019).

# A PARTIAL LIST OF SNUGGLY BOOKS

www.ingramcontent.com/pod-product-compliance
Lightning Source LLC
Chambersburg PA
CBHW050318110726
47899CB00007B/2286